THE
ASPARAGUS
BUNCH

THE ASPARAGUS BUNCH

JESSICA SCOTT-WHYTE

WELBECK
FLAME

Published in 2022 by Welbeck Flame
An imprint of Welbeck Children's Limited,
part of Welbeck Publishing Group.
Based in London and Sydney.
www.welbeckpublishing.com

ISBN: 978 1 80130 046 9

Designed by Perfect Bound Ltd
Printed and bound by CPI Group (UK)

10 9 8 7 6 5 4 3 2 1

MIX
Paper from
responsible sources
FSC® C171272

For Carmel (Nana) and the Thornton family
of Kilmacud, Dublin 14. For everything.

Introduction

(The completely pointless part that nobody reads)

This is a waste of time.

Chances are you've already snuck a peek at the last chapter and know how the whole thing ends, so what good is an introduction to you now?

My 'we're kind of a big deal' book publisher, however, insisted they knew better and said that I had to write an introduction – no ifs, ands or buts.

I told them they were delusional and that there was no way I could write an introduction without using the words *if, and* or *but*. Then they got cross and told me I had an attitude problem.

So, here's my introduction:

Hello.
My name is Leon.
I have an attitude problem.

1
The Basics

Everything you need to know about me:
1. I'm Leon John Crothers
2. I'm 4,779 days old (13 years and 1 month, if you're mathematically challenged)
3. I live with Caroline
4. I've been moved on from 6 different schools
5. I'm currently attending Deluney College (school #7)
6. Most people think I've got an attitude problem

Everything you need to know about Caroline:
1. Caroline Angela Crothers is my mum
2. I call Caroline by her first name
3. Caroline doesn't mind that I call her by her first name
4. Caroline is, among other things, a single parent, a whistler, a knitter and an indiscreet nosepicker
5. Caroline rides fairground attractions for a living
6. Caroline doesn't think I've got an attitude problem

Everything you need to know about my attitude problem:

1. It has nothing to do with the fact that I'm from Blackpool
2. Or my squeaky noise phobia
3. Or my deep hatred of baked beans
4. Or that I own 14 identical yellow hoodies
5. Or my opinions on trainspotters
6. Or how I eat my Cadbury Creme Egg

2
Soggy Chips

Tea at ours is very straightforward.

Tea meaning dinner if you're not from round here.

You see, Caroline's a hopeless cook.

As soon as I was old enough to coherently tell her this, I took matters into my own hands:

Monday: Fish and chips
Tuesday: Chicken and chips
Wednesday: Pizza and chips
Thursday: Egg and chips
Friday: Sausage and chips
Saturday: Steak and chips
Sunday: Curry and chips

I wouldn't call myself a picky eater. I'm just not keen on surprises. And Caroline isn't keen on me skipping meals, so this way, everyone's a winner.

And as we're on the subject of meals, maybe just a quick word about the chips.

I eat my chips plain (no ketchup, vinegar, mayonnaise etc. – only salt) and they can't touch any other foods on the plate. It generates stress. Unnecessary stress. Don't waste your time wondering why I don't just eat my chips from a separate plate – spare me. Been there, hated that.

As I was saying, tea at ours is very straightforward.

I always sit beside the kitchen door with my back to the shelf where Caroline keeps her collection of ceramic ducks, because they're hideous, and Caroline sits at ninety degrees to my right. Over the years, I've encouraged Caroline to sit there so that she'd have a nice view out of the kitchen window but really, I just don't like her sitting directly opposite me at mealtimes. I don't like anyone sitting opposite me at mealtimes. Who needs to see all that chewing and swallowing? Listening to it is bad enough.

Conversation is to be kept to a strict minimum. It drags out the eating process. For me, eating is really more of a hassle than anything else and something I prefer to do alone. I only eat at all because if I don't, my vital organs will eventually stage a mutiny. Caroline has a thing about the two of us eating together whenever her work schedule allows, for 'bonding' purposes. In the past, this has been a frequent source of arguing, but we've finally come to, what I think, is a fair compromise: mealtimes spent together – ask only about the weather.

So, like I said, tea at ours is very straightforward.

My story, however, is anything but straightforward and starts right here.

To give you a more accurate timeframe, it was a Monday evening, two weeks before I was due to start at Deluney College: my new, new, new, new, new, new, new school.

The two of us were making our way through our fish and chips in relative silence, when suddenly, out of nowhere, Caroline said the strangest thing:

'I'm worried about you.'

I quickly scanned my plate to see if she was referring to a runaway chip situation, but everything seemed in order, so I just carried on eating.

Caroline cleared her throat.

'Leon, I was thinking that before you start at your new school, you—'

'Correction: new, new, new, new, new, new, new school.'

'OK, before you start at your new, new, new, new, new, new, new school, it might be a good idea that we go and see someone who helps young people who've trouble making friends and, well, interacting with people in general. What do you think?'

I stabbed a piece of battered fish with my fork.

'No thanks, Caroline.'

Case closed, I figured. Caroline had asked a question (albeit a non-weather-related one) and I'd answered. But the same question came back again the following night over breaded chicken, and *again* on Wednesday between mouthfuls of margherita. Normally I wouldn't describe Caroline as annoying, but this new teatime routine was pinching a nerve.

Then, on Thursday, she changed tactics:

'I've made an appointment for you to see Dr Snot on Saturday afternoon.'

I looked up from my egg and chips.

'What?'

'On Saturday afternoon you've an appointment to see Dr Snot.'

'Dr Snot?'

'Snot.'

'It's not.'

'What?'

'*Snot.*'

'Yep. Snot.'

'Dr *Snot*?'

Caroline knew full well I'd fall for her plan. If someone tells you there's a man alive with a name as stupid as Dr Snot, of course you're going to go and see him. You're *obliged* to. The conversation was now distracting me to the point that some of the yolk from my egg had dripped off my fork onto my chips. Beads of sweat were forming on my forehead and my elbows were starting to itch.

'*Fine*, Caroline, I'll go and see him,' I said, as I scraped my food into the bin.

3
Dr Snot

Two days later, we were sitting in the waiting room of Dr Snot's surgery. Caroline passed the time with a stack of sticky magazines that she'd picked up from the reception desk, while I tapped my chin with my index finger to the rhythm of the clock that was mounted on the wall.

When we were finally invited into his office, Dr Snot was sitting behind his big, brown, shiny doctor's desk, wearing a white doctor's coat and a pair of ugly doctor's glasses. He was bald, with some wiry grey hair sticking out of his ears, an unhealthy-sized belly and a few too many moles on his face. He basically looked like your average, close-to-retirement physician. *Complete* disappointment.

I turned to leave.

'What are you doing?' said Caroline, nudging me back in. 'We just got here.'

'You said you wanted me to go and see Dr Snot,' I answered. 'I've seen him, so I can go now, right?'

She sighed heavily. 'Leon, I didn't mean to go and see him, *literally*.'

'It's all right, Ms Crothers,' said Dr Snot, with an impressively deep voice. 'Lovely to meet you, Leon, and thanks for taking the time to come all this way just to have a look at me. Good to see that you're a lad who keeps his word!'

We sat down.

'Snot isn't really your last name, is it?' I said.

'Beg your pardon?' said the doc.

'Which controversial family tree are you trying to distance yourself from?'

'*Leon*,' Caroline hissed under her breath.

'Was your grandfather Hitler's secret love child or something?'

'Leon!' Caroline shrieked.

I threw my eyes down to the floor. When Caroline's voice gets loud it means I've said something that's likely to have caused upset, anger or offence.

'Sor-ry,' I told my shoes. 'I may have said something that has caused upset, anger or offence.'

I waited a moment for the expected '*listen here, young man*' speech but none came, so I looked up at Dr Snot, who was leaning over his desk with his hands cupped under his chin. He was smiling.

'Tell me, Leon, what do you think of Milky Ways?'

Now I was *really* confused.

'Are you questioning the meaning of life?' I asked him. 'Or are you planning to take up astronomy as a hobby when you retire?'

'No, no, the chocolate bar!' the snot doc laughed. 'Did you know that Milky Ways have been a favourite of mine since I was a young—'

'The Milky Way bar is a chocolate-covered confectionery bar with a nougat centre, manufactured and distributed by the Mars confectionery company. It was created in 1923 by Frank C. Mars after the famed malted milk drink (milkshake) of the day, which was in turn named after the Earth's galaxy. The American version of the Milky Way bar has a caramel and nougat filling, while the European version has just an airy nougat filling. The Milky Way's low density of 0.88 grams per centimetre cubed means it floats when placed in milk, a phenomenon that was used for an advertising campaign across Europe in the late 1980s.'

'Very impressive,' said the doc. 'Your mother had already mentioned to me on the phone that you had a great passion for the world of confectionery. Who knows? Maybe someday you'll be the next Willy Wonka!'

The doc got up from his chair and squeezed himself around the side of his desk.

'Leon, I would like that you and your mother come back and see me next week for a chat, before school starts. Would that be OK?'

'Not a chance,' I said. 'Willy Wonka's a fictional character in literature with lunatic tendencies who exploited ingenious dwarfs as slave labourers and was a few Everlasting Gobstoppers away from being charged with infanticide.'

Caroline hurried me out of my chair.

'OK, Leon, let's be off.'

I stood up.

'Keep in mind, Dr Snot, that the American version of the Milky Way bar contains 240 calories in each 52.2-gram bar, while the British version only contains 95 calories. I say that because you're visibly overweight, so you might—'

Caroline yanked my hoodie.

'Leon… hop to it. Now.'

'That went better than expected,' I said to Caroline as I pogoed out of the doc's office on one foot.

4
My Hobby

Author disclosure: I haven't consented to the publication of this chapter for the following reasons:

1. Against my wishes, the chapter's initial 22-page count has been ludicrously reduced
2. I wasn't allowed to include any pie charts, line graphs, histograms or frequency polygons
3. This book has been edited by someone whose chocolate bar of choice is a **Bounty** – enough said

Carnival folk generally have a reputation for being dodgy swindlers who'll hack off their heavily tattooed right arms to make a few quid. But it also must be said that carnies are very loyal and protective of their people. So, when Caroline showed up to work at Blackpool Pleasure Beach, one day way back when, with a newborn baby in her arms (nine months after being hired to test-ride the dodgems), they treated me as one of their own. In fact, I quickly became a sort of side-show attraction within the carny community along the promenade.

Anytime I'd toddle past a stand or a booth, a hooked finger would beckon me closer and a sweet would be dropped into the front pocket of my red corduroy dungarees.

Thanks to what can only be described as a spectacular show of parental negligence (kudos, Caroline), my constant access to processed sugar uncovered in me a rare talent that landed me my first ever paid job at age four: taste-testing bootleg fairground sweets to see if they were near, past or way past their sell by date. I was paid £1 for every stash I sampled, with a £5 bonus if I managed to detect that a stash had been infiltrated by vermin. I used the money I made (and trust me, I made *a lot*) to expand my confectionery knowledge beyond the realms of fairground fare. Today, scoffing sweets from around the world, be it through chewing, chomping, licking, sucking, munching, or crunching, is my life's calling.

Caroline childishly calls it my hobby.

Nowhere near everything you need to know about my hobby:

1. My pursuit of sweetness has already seen two near-death experiences. Some years back, I almost choked during a tasting experiment involving a mouthful of bullseyes and only last summer, a piece of saltwater taffy got lodged in my throat and had to be removed in A&E using forceps.
2. The results of my in-depth study into jawbreakers,

conducted four years ago, remain inconclusive. I was forced to abandon the study after cracking two of my back molars, but I plan to resurrect and complete the project when I'm in my seventies and have a reliable set of porcelain false gnashers.

3. The most Chupa Chups lollipops I've consumed in a day is 27, which caused me to lose all feeling in my cheeks and I couldn't eat solids for six days straight.

4. Have you ever noticed that the chocolate bars you eat from Christmas selection boxes don't taste the same as the ones you buy at any other time of the year? I'm convinced that confectionery companies alter the recipes of selection box chocolates to create a unique feeling of festive nostalgia in a bid to pump up sales. That's just one of many sweet-natured conspiracy theories that has my name on it.

5. I always taste-test new sweets between 7 and 8 in the morning, just before breakfast. Did you know that saliva builds up in your mouth throughout the day and can dramatically change the flavour profile of whatever you're eating?

6. A side occupation of my 'hobby' includes collecting rare confectionery memorabilia, which I store in a glass cabinet above my bed. Special items include the original prototype of the chocolate frog candy used in the film adaptation of *Harry Potter and the*

Philosopher's Stone, and a glass bonbon dish recovered from the wreckage of the *Titanic*.

7. For the past three years, I've been working on an algorithm to determine the best sweet combinations that make up £2 worth of pick 'n' mix. The best combination I've got so far is: 2 large strawbs, 4 sour dummies, 3 white mice, 6 fried eggs, 4 fizzy cola bottles, 3 flying saucers and 1 red liquorice wheel.

8. I'm currently campaigning for Starburst sweets to be re-released as their original brand name: Opal Fruits. So far, my online petition has generated 18,000 signatures.

9. I eat my Cadbury Creme Egg by first bashing the top off against a hard surface, before sucking out the fondant filling with my tongue and throwing away the remaining shell, just as any respectful egg predator in the animal kingdom would.

10. Thanks to Love Hearts, I learnt to read way before the average kid.

So, there you have it, a very brief glimpse into the epicentre of my world. After reading this, you might be intrigued, possibly inspired, and so you should be.

Anyone who thinks otherwise can just fudge off.

5
Denial

I was adamant that I'd never hop in *or* out of Dr Snot's surgery ever again, but you'd be amazed what a lad will do to not have his annual subscription to *International Confectionery* magazine cancelled.

The doc received us with his usual jolly expression. I wore my hoodie backwards and kept the hood up – my attempt at a protest.

'Thanks to both of you for coming back to speak with me,' the doc began. 'It's nice to see you again, Leon.'

'See me?' I muffled through the yellow cotton fibres. 'So, you've acquired laser vision since we last spoke, Doc?'

'Hmm. Tell me, Leon, how have things been this past week? I imagine you've been enjoying the last few days of summer before—'

'Doc, you and I both know that we aren't here to engage in polite chit-chat, so if you could make a conscious effort to hurry things along…'

Caroline started wriggling uncomfortably in her chair. 'Leon, you *promised* me you wouldn't go off on one.'

'And *you* promised *me* that you'd never put chocolate in the fridge. How many times has that one fallen flat?'

'Only on very hot days. No big deal.'

'No big deal?! It drastically modifies the molecular structure of the cocoa. You may as well be throwing it in the bin!'

'If I may?' interrupted the doc. 'OK, Leon, I'll get to the point. Having looked extensively at your *numerous* school files, having exchanged at length with your mum and former teachers and having met also with you in person, I am inclined to think that you have an autism spectrum disorder.'

What did he just say?

Cue prolonged silence, during which Caroline's reddening cheeks sent out guilt-ridden distress signals before she eventually cracked under the pressure.

'Gosh. Erm… could you explain this disorder to us, Doctor?'

Oh, this was rich.

I pulled down my hood.

'Caroline, do me a favour and stop pretending as if you don't already know every word that's going to come out of *that* man's mouth. The two of you have clearly been in cahoots from the very beginning!'

I swivelled my head deskward.

'For your information, Docky Snotty, for as long as I can remember, people have told me that I've got an attitude problem. *I* know that's completely false and up until eighteen seconds ago, I was under the impression that Caroline was in agreement. To me, that's all that's ever mattered: everyone else is wrong, Caroline and I know better. And I'm happy it stays that way.'

'Unfair' wasn't the word. This was an out-and-out sham. A hold-up. I bet the diploma on this old fogy's wall was a load of fraudulent gobbledygook printed on the back of a Nando's menu.

'Leon, you *don't* have an attitude problem, let me make that clear,' said the doc. 'What I do believe you have, however, are many characteristics of someone who has autism. Now, to put it simply, autism is a developmental disability that affects how people communicate and interact with the world around them.'

'*Disability*? So, I'm disabled now, am I? Great. I can't think of a better way to start my weekend.'

'I understand that this might be a lot to take in, Leon, so let's take things step by step. Today, we speak about autism being a spectrum disorder because it is a condition that affects people in different ways and in varying degrees. But all people on the autism spectrum share some common traits, such as having difficulty with social interaction and communication. They tend to have a strict need for sameness and can display repetitive patterns of behaviour, such as the food they eat for example. It is often the case that they are particularly sensitive to certain lights, sounds, tastes and smells. And it is also common that they have highly focused interests or hobbies.'

'Unbelievable. So, what fancy label do I get suckered to my face then in that case? Damaged goods? Fragile – handle with care? Approach with caution?'

'*None* of the above. You know, Leon, many well-known people in history are thought to have been on the autistic spectrum.'

'Oh yeah? Such as?'

'Well, Mozart, for example.'

'Mozart was composing music at age five, Doc. I'm already thirteen, so if you're trying to suggest that one day I could equal his chart-topping legacy, we're eight years behind schedule, easily.'

'Every autism case is different, Leon. Albert Einstein is also presumed to have been on the autistic spectrum. He won the Nobel Prize for Physics and is probably the world's most famous scientist, yet he barely uttered a word for the first three years of his life.'

'He's also a mass murderer.'

'Excuse me?'

'Einstein. $E=MC^2$. The atomic bomb. Hiroshima. Two hundred thousand death toll. More like E=MC screwed.'

'Leon—'

'Or E=MC sayonara, suckers.'

'All right, Leon, let's continue… Charles Darwin: the world's most beloved biologist.'

'Otherwise known as the world's most beloved heretic.'

'Well now—'

'Doc, did he or did he not go against all world religions in stating that man was descended from monkeys? Besides, all your examples are purely speculative. You may as well say that Santa Claus is autistic because he kept obsessive lists of children's names and refused to eat anything accept milk and cookies.

'In that case, what about Greta Thunberg? She's a terrific ambassador for this generation's autistic community.'

'Greta Thunberg? The doomsday girl? Next.'

'OK then, I've another interesting one for you: Satoshi Tajiri.'

'Abuser.'

'Are you suggesting that the creator of the Pokémon franchise is an—'

'Doc, as the brainchild of Pokémon, he's solely responsible for fostering and feeding the gaming addictions of tens of millions of adults and kids worldwide. If that's not a form of abuse, I don't know what is.'

Dr Snot leant forward in his chair.

'Leon, while science has made significant advances in understanding autism these past decades, unfortunately the same cannot always be said for how people *view* autism. There is still a lot of misunderstanding out there. In the past, people were led to believe that being autistic meant that a person's brain wasn't functioning properly. What we now know today proves the opposite. People on the autistic spectrum have brains that function *differently*. And let me tell you something: seeing and understanding things differently to others is by *no* means a bad thing. If anything, it gives you a cognitive uniqueness that others don't have and never will have.'

I put my hood back up over my face.

'Let's go, Caroline.'

'But Leon, we haven't—'

'Let's go, Caroline.'

'Leon, listen to me,' stressed Dr Snot. 'If you take away one thing from our conversation, please let it be this: *there is nothing wrong with you.'*

'My thoughts precisely, Doc,' I replied as I threw open the door to his office. 'Good to see that our diagnoses are aligned. Please note that I'll be sending you a bill for the forty-six minutes you've taken off my life for explaining the fudging obvious.'

6
De Looney Bin

Everything you need to know about Deluney College:
1. The walls of the building are brown brick
2. The floors of the building are brown tiles
3. The uniforms are 100% polyester
4. The trays in the canteen are very sticky
5. The hand dryer in the boys' toilets is out of service
6. The headmaster could be Winston Churchill's identical twin

It's often said that the first day at a new school can be daunting, intimidating, even nerve-wrecking. For me, the experience has become an overwhelming case of déjà vu (that's French, for those of you *qui ne parlez-pas français*).

So, while most first-dayers walk through the halls with trepidation, worrying who will be their new best friend for life, which teachers will inspire them to embark on an academic road to excellence, I wonder about who or what will be the reason for my foreseen departure.

Because here's the thing: I'm *not* the reason that I've been moved on from six different schools. That's the absolute truth. I'm even happy to give you the details.

Reasons I was moved on from my previous schools:
1. St. Edmund's National School — wooden flooring and a load of brown brogue shoes. Sometimes, late at night, I'm still woken up by the sound of the squeaking.
2. St. Mary's Comprehensive — total case of false advertising. None of the teaching staff were comprehensive, *at all*.
3. St. Tiernan's Community College — their woollen-blend school jackets were so itchy that I was one scratching episode away from a skin graft.
4. Mount Sackville College — yes, I'm quite in agreement that the school's incompetent headmaster, Mr Dempsey, should indeed be given the sack.
5. Holy Child Community School — it didn't take me long to see the light. Literally. The 100W bulbs they used in every single light fixture burned my eyes from the second I arrived in the place.
6. Dartmoor Hall — affectionately known as the Hogwarts of the North-West, but I can confirm there was absolutely nothing magical about its academic standards whatsoever.

Anyway, back to Deluney College... also known as De Looney Bin, according to toilet cubicle scripture.

After a welcome ramble from the headmaster, who wished me much success in my new scholastic venture, I tried with little success to stick out an entire geography class with a *very* talkative teacher who spoke with a lisp. Not only that, she had a sinus infection. Needless to say, my head was melted by the end of the lesson.

Maths was equally stressful. The teacher kept using the word 'basically' when explaining the equation solutions on the board. I calculated that in the space of forty-four minutes, he said the word 'basically' seventy-six times… which led me to conclude that he was basically a donkey.

Next came science – nothing major to report, except that the teacher's legs were riddled with varicose veins. That had me thinking of Pot Noodles until the bell rang.

In keeping with tradition, I went home for dinner (otherwise known as lunch, if you're not a card-carrying Northerner): a banana sandwich, a banana and a glass of milk. It's the same dinner I've eaten every day since I started school, age five. Caroline always cribs about the fact that I insist on eating my banana sandwich with a knife and fork, because it gives her more washing up to do. I always make a point of reminding her that by not eating with my hands, I don't use up any hand soap, so it's a case of equals smequals.

Back in time for history, where I pretty much zoned out, except for a brief moment when I realised that our lesson about Spanish explorer Hernán Cortés's conquering of the

Aztec Empire between 1519 and 1521 failed to mention that it was Cortés who brought back an Aztec cocoa bean drink with him to Spain and presented it to King Charles the Fifth, thus igniting the Western world's obsession with chocolate. No biggie, you'll say.

I was looking forward to the next lesson. During his welcome speech, the headmaster had said that he'd organised for one of my fellow school chumps to give me a tour of the building during English class. I'd no interest in the tour or speaking to a random person for a prolonged stretch of time, but both options seemed way better than sitting in front of my new English teacher: a buck-toothed walrus who smelt of cigarettes and a Greggs sausage roll.

So, after history, I dutifully plonked myself down on the bench outside the school secretary's office and waited. Just who was going to disgrace me with their presence? Boy or girl? Geek or freak? Enemy or nemesis?

'Hi, I'm Tanya.'

The first thing I saw was the Afro.

It was a good thing she'd said her name *before* I'd looked up from my phone, or it wouldn't have registered with me at all. Honestly, she could have called herself Mary Christmas and I wouldn't have batted an eyelid.

Initially, I just stared at her, until she was obliged to ask, 'Eh, you gotta name then?'

My brain was still too preoccupied to make words,

so I resorted to holding up my phone cover, which has a customised Lion bar logo that reads 'Leon' instead of 'Lion'. One of Caroline's better unrequested birthday presents.

Her nose wrinkled as she studied the logo.

'The headmaster asked one of us in class to show you around, so I said I'd do it. Anything to get out of English. *Hate* English.'

'It's funny how schools nowadays make a big fuss about kids not being allowed to dye their hair blue or shave their back and sides like a mullet, but they turn a blind eye to the disco bush.'

'What?'

'Their reasoning is completely biased. How can they say that having barbed wire inked around your neck or a bullring dangling from your septum is distracting, but that having a hairstyle that makes your head look like a microphone isn't? Quite honestly, Afros are *very* distracting, plus they can visibly impair somebody who's stuck behind one in class and can't see the lesson on the board.'

Then she scrunched up her face at me.

I immediately put into practice Caroline's tried and tested

advice: scrunched-up faces, reverse two paces.

'What are you doing?' she asked.

'I might have said something that has caused anger, offence or upset.'

'Ya think?'

'Well, according to popular opinion, what I just said wasn't very socio-politically correct. You know the saying: Afro = no-go.'

'No kidding. Personally I'm not big on racist comments, especially after lunch.'

'Just to be clear, I'm not racist.'

'Oh really?'

'Yes.'

'Well in that case you're seriously ignorant. Look, in this place, you're either fat, or ugly, or spotty, or smelly, or stupid; they'll always tag you with something. It's part of the deal, if you like. So, I'd watch yourself, if I were you. You're gobby, and if there's one thing they don't like round here, it's a newbie with a big gob.'

'They?'

'The tough lads.'

'Of course, no educational establishment would be complete without a resident gang of troublemakers. And I suppose they have a ringleader, do they?'

'Glen Jenkins. No, seriously, stay away from that lad. He's a proper nutcase. D'you know that before his family moved up here from Leeds, he'd been kicked out of, like, four different schools?'

'That's quite something, all right. Thanks for the warning.'

'What school were you at before coming here?'

'Some stuffy boarding school in the Scottish Highlands,' I lied. 'My mum thought that the mountain air would be good for me, but it turns out I'm severely allergic to heather shrubs, so there was a change of plan.'

'Was that your mum who dropped you off this morning, in the white van?'

'Yes.'

'The one with the mad-looking woolly coat?'

'Caroline's a keen knitter.'

'I saw her talking to the headmaster just before assembly. She was telling him about some diagnosis you have. You all right?'

'Caroline's recently been led to believe that I may have some brain abnormality, which comes with a whimsical name and a whole lot of pointless fuss.'

'What's it called?'

'Snot…'

'What?'

'He thought he was so clever reciting that slick speech in his office about me having an autism spectrum disorder… he didn't think for one minute that I'd fact-check. Turns out that what he *actually* thinks I have is Asperger syndrome.'

'Asa-what?'

'Asperger's. Back in the 1940s, an Austrian psychiatrist named Hans Asperger found that people could actually be autistic without their language or intelligence being affected. The term Asperger syndrome was then used to identify those specific autism cases. Trouble is, the man was also a Swastika-worshipping Nazi. Of course, the doc managed to leave *that* minor detail out of his speech… there's a surprise.'

'Eh, what's the name again of that thing you've got?'

'I haven't "got" anything. I'm perfectly fine.'

'Then why was your mum saying to the headmaster that—'

'*Because* a doctor with a fake last name managed to get his pudgy hands on her frontal lobe. The poor woman is easily coerced by men in positions of authority. That's what happens when you spend your university years in a travelling cult.'

'A cult? You serious?'

I wish.

'Today, her critical thinking processes are as good as extinct. Do you guys have a tuck shop?'

'No, just a machine. It's down the end of the corridor, on the left. I can take you if you want?'

'OK, fine.'

She started off down the corridor.

'This way, Noel.'

Noel?

'My name's Leon.'

'Oh, yeah. Sorry.'

I trailed behind her slightly so that I could discreetly ogle her bag but apparently I wasn't being as discreet as I thought.

'Something wrong with my bag?' she asked.

'No. It's just, the pattern on it reminds me of a jar of jazzies.'

'I *love* jazzies. They're my absolute favourite! Chocolate buttons covered in loadsa them little round sprinkle thingies. I mean, what's not to like?'

A phantom shiver rippled down my spine. *Jazzies*? Of all the sweets in the entire world (even localised to Blackpool, where there's already a staggering variety), jazzies are her favourite? The very same as *me*? Well, if I'm being honest, they're probably tied first place with Toblerones, but that's another story altogether.

We reached the end of the corridor and I turned left.

'Oi, Noel, it's this way.'

'You said left at the end of the corridor.'

'Yeah, I know. You're going the wrong way.'

'But this way is left, you're about to turn right.'

'Whatever, it's this way. Follow me.'

Strange.

When we arrived at the vending machine, I stopped a few paces short, closed my eyes and stood with my back to it.

'From left to right, top to bottom: Dairy Milk, Snickers, Bounty, Flake, Twirl, Mars, Twix, Kit Kat, Kit Kat Chunky, Galaxy, Aero, Wispa, Double Decker, Yorkie, Lion bar.'

I opened my eyes again and saw Tanya staring back at me with a face like a guppy fish.

'Eh, are you for real?'

'What?'

'No, for real, what planet are we on?'

Her reaction really wasn't what I was expecting.

'Eh, Planet Earth?'

'Are you like big into vending machines or something? Are you American?'

'I'm not American. And what has being American got to do with liking vending machines?'

'Well, they've got a lot of 'em over there, haven't they? They probably invented them.'

'The first ever vending machine dates back to ancient Egypt. A Greek engineer and mathematician, Hero of Alexandria, invented a coin-operated instrument to stop churchgoers from stealing holy water. The device was triggered by the weight of a gold coin, which allowed a vessel to tip and a measure of water to flow out for ritual washing in Egyptian temples.'

Tanya blinked slowly. 'You *sure* we're on Planet Earth right now?'

'Yes.'

'OK, well whatever floats your boat, I guess.'

What boat?

She walked slowly around the vending machine. 'These things are so boring-looking. I mean, you'd think that in this day and age, they'd have to come up with something funkier looking than a black fridge.'

'You're just saying that because you haven't been exposed to the more advanced vending machine concepts that exist in the world,' I explained. 'From Japanese vending machines for example, you can buy flower arrangements, board games, fishing bait, even live puppies. Japan has the highest number of vending machines per capita in the world, one for every twenty-three inhabitants, meaning just under five million vending machines.'

'So, I take it you're not gonna buy anything from this machine, then?'

'No. I should probably get going. I'm meeting someone down at the seafront.'

'You not coming to P.E?'

Time for another lie. 'I recently strained my left Achilles tendon in a freak water-skiing accident in Barbados. It's still fragile.'

'Right so,' she said. 'If you're taking a bus into town, you're better off using the side entrance to the school. Go back the way we came, turn right, then right again, and it will be on your left.'

'Thanks.'

'See ya, Noel.'

Two right turns and a left turn later, standing in front of the disabled toilets with no building exit in sight, I couldn't help but feel that something was definitely amiss.

7

Conversations with Caroline

'Maggie, have you seen Caroline?'

The old woman's murky eyes turned slowly in my direction. They were barely visible under the large folds of her face flesh. She coughed deeply and I could hear the tar-soaked mucus sloshing about in her lungs.

Maggie is a bona fide freak of nature. In all the years that I've been visiting Caroline at work, she's been sitting behind the same plush toy stand, glued to her fold-out chair like a limpet. Sometimes, I wonder whether she just sleeps sitting upright, right there in the heart of Blackpool Pleasure Beach, in all weather conditions.

'Up the Big One,' she husked.

I carried on past the SpongeBob Splash Bash, turned left at Avalanche, before easing my way through the giddy small talk coming from the queue that snaked towards the Big One. In typical fashion, Caroline's kumquat-coloured hair was flapping around the front wagon as the roller coaster hurtled along its tracks. A text came through mid-circuit:

Think I c u. Down in a tick.

'You hungry?' she asked when the ride had finished. 'I can grab you some candy floss.'

'Not necessary. You?'

'Nah. The tuna sandwich I had earlier keeps trying to climb back up the way it came for some reason, the cheeky chappie.'

Caroline had to test the Derby Racer ride next, so she suggested I join her for a full retelling of day one at my new, new, new, new, new, new, new school.

As soon as our horses were on the move, I launched into a full-blown monologue, making a point of going into great detail so that Caroline wouldn't miss out on anything important. She halted me after four minutes.

'As much as I'm thrilled to hear all about your new school's—'

'Correction—'

'OK, OK, new-times-seven school's *vending machine*, I was hoping to hear a bit more about your actual *day* at school. What were the teachers like?'

'Underwhelming, overopinionated. Same old, same old.'

'Anything else?'

'The floors are tiled. Pleasant surprise.'

'Anything else?'

'No.'

'Nothing?'

'I spoke to a girl.'

Caroline lunged forward. 'Leon, you spoke to somebody? You spoke to a girl?'

'Not intentionally. She started the conversation.'

'That's incredible, Leon, I can't believe it!' Caroline gushed. 'Well, go on then, tell me more about her!'

'There's nothing to say really. I'm currently trying to work out whether she's an incognito bully or someone who's quite a few brain cells short of a basic intelligence level.'

'Where are you getting that from?'

'Her behaviour was suspicious.'

'*Suspicious?*'

'Well for one thing, she clearly doesn't know her left from her right.'

'Anyone can make that kind of—'

'She didn't know that she was living on Planet Earth, Caroline.'

'Are you sure?'

'I had to reassure her more than once.'

'Well—'

'She also called me Noel, Caroline. On a number of occasions.'

'Forgetting a person's name when you meet them for the first time can—'

'Initially I was leaning towards the bully hypothesis, but it doesn't explain the Planet Earth absurdity and her blatant unawareness at confusing her right with her left. I'm more inclined to think that the girl's just very stupid. Pity. At least it doesn't seem to bother her. I'll just make an effort to avoid her as much as possible and suffer the occasional "Hey, Noel" misaddress.'

'Maybe it's a nickname?'

'A nickname, Caroline? After knowing each other a few minutes?'

'Or perhaps you remind her of a Noel that she knows? That's happened to me before, getting names and faces mixed up.'

The combination of talking and spinning was starting to unsettle my mental equilibrium. I closed my eyes and tried to tune in to some white noise to calm myself. It didn't work for very long; a strange sound that you could liken to an ambulance siren was increasing in volume not far from where we were seated.

'Le-on?'

'*Le-on*?'

'*LE-ON*?'

My eyes opened reluctantly.

'What, Caroline?'

'Why are you always not answering me on purpose?'

'Why would I bother to answer to my own name when you are sitting less than a metre from me? You're better off just saying whatever it is you want to say and, with any luck, if what you say is interesting or pertinent, I'll respond.'

'Well, I was going to say that you probably remind her of that famous rockstar from the nineties with the same haircut as you. Noel… oh, what's his name? Big bushy eyebrows. He was in a band with his brother. What were they called again? Something like a fruity cocktail.'

'Noel Gallagher? As in the former songwriter, lead guitarist and co-lead vocalist of the rock band Oasis? Current lead vocalist, guitarist and songwriter for Noel Gallagher's High Flying Birds?'

'Spot on! How did you know that? You've never been into music much and Oasis is a bit before your time.'

'Two summers ago, I was researching the history and heritage of Quality Street chocolates. Noel Gallagher's name came up in an online search. He'd said in an interview that, according to him, the perfectly brewed cup of tea *must* be the colour of a Quality Street toffee sweet inside its yellow wrapper. I thought it was a very insightful remark. I did a backcheck on him. Interesting bloke. From the lyrics I've read on Wiki, his songs seem quite decent too.'

'Why don't you ask your friend about him then the next time you see her?'

'Tanya's not a friend.'

'Ah! So, her name's Tanya?'

'Supposedly. Although if her planetary confusion is anything to go by, she could well be a cyborg named Tron from the planet Neptune. All I know is that, right now. I'm keeping my options open.'

8
Unpleasantness

My second day at Deluney started off pretty well. I didn't oversleep, my fingers didn't wrinkle in the shower, I dug out a very satisfying nugget of wax from my left ear canal *and* I managed to salvage a full bowl of Special K from what was left in the packet, leaving Caroline with the crumbly dregs. I didn't even have to run for the bus.

Of course, once I'd crossed the threshold of the brown-bricked building, things took a nosedive.

The unpleasantness began just before the morning bell, when I was taking some books out of my locker.

'Asparagus!'

I turned around. Nobody stood out from the lines of moving bodies pushing their way up and down the corridor, so, I carried on arranging my things.

'All right, Asparagus?'

'Oi! Asparagus!'

'As-pa-ra-gus!'

I turned around again, now fairly sure that these veggie taunts were being directed at me, but nobody materialised.

With the clock seconds from striking late, I wedged the incident to the back of my mind and headed to class.

Everyone was already at their desks when I arrived, but as luck would have it, my chain-smoking, sausage-roll-scoffing English teacher waddled into class at the same moment I did, so she didn't make an example of me. As I took my seat, I spotted Tanya down the back of the classroom. She was surrounded by a group of lads who looked like they fell into the 'troublemaker' category.

Tanya smiled at me discreetly. I didn't smile back. The troublemakers were now watching my every move. It's probably worth mentioning that even if they had ignored me completely, I still wouldn't have smiled back at Tanya. I'm not one for facial expressions in general.

I turned back around and faced the front of the class as the register began.

'Claire Abrahams… Tanya Asher… Paul Barkley… Gregory Bates… Tina Coleman… Leon Crothers…'

'ASPARAGUS!'

The entire class burst out laughing.

'Glen Jenkins, settle down. I'll be having none of that,' the teacher wheezed, still out of breath from her car-to-classroom commute.

Surprise, surprise. Glen Jenkins had emerged as the chief perpetrator. Day two in my new, new, new, new, new, new, new school and I was already in deep, deep, deep, deep, deep,

deep, deep Snickers.

'Miss, I'm not disturbin',' Glen said in a street accent that could curdle milk. 'I was just pointin' out that there's an erra on yer list. Our new lad's name 'ere's not Leon, Miss. It's As-para-gus.'

The laughing intensified.

'Mr Jenkins—'

'Am I right, Tanya? It's As-para-gus, innit?'

I glanced over my shoulder at Tanya, who was looking in my direction and making an awkward face, as if words were causing a traffic jam in her mouth.

'MR JENKINS! THAT'S ENOUGH!'

I spent the rest of the lesson in a dream-like state, replaying the conversation I'd had with Tanya over and over again in my mind. To be honest, the signs *were* all there. She was trying to come across as aloof and ditzy, when in fact she was on a solo mission to carry out Glen Jenkins' orders: suss out the new kid and then report back to Bully HQ for a full debrief. It had all the makings of a blockbuster movie: *The Spy Who Slagged Me*.

As soon as class had ended, I speedily gathered my stuff and headed straight for my locker, only to find that it had been broken into. *ASPARAGUS* had been scrawled across all my books and, with particular thoughtfulness, someone had taken all the pens from my pencil case and replaced them with asparagus spears.

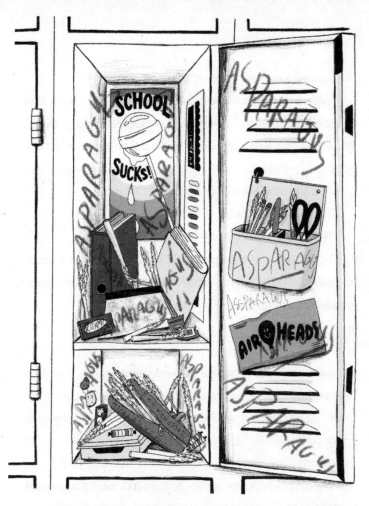

Rage was now elbowing its way through my bloodstream and the veins in my temples were throbbing.

'Noel?'

Unbelievable. She actually had the balls to come and speak to me after having assisted in my public humiliation just moments before? I swear, the sound of her voice made me want to puncture my own eardrums.

'Go away, Tanya,' I said with my back to her.

'Listen, Noel, there's been a *huge* mistake.'

'Of course there has. No explanation required, though. Luckily, I'm not a simpleton. I've worked things out for myself. Spare me the details and go back to pressing your lips firmly onto Glen's sweaty bum-cheeks.'

'What you on about?'

'Be gone, Judas.'

'Look, just hear me out, would ya? Yesterday during P.E I was talking to Claire, you know, Claire who's in our class, and, well, I kinda told her about your asparagus thingy. I know it wasn't right to say anything to her without you knowing, and, well, typical Claire, she's gone repeating it even though I *told* her not to, and it's all gone a bit mental. I'm really sorry, Noel. Like, *proper* sorry.'

I slammed my locker shut and spun around. 'Asparagus?'

'Yeah?'

'*Asparagus*?'

'Yeah… you know that thingy you were on about yesterday.'

'Hmm. Funny, I don't have the slightest recollection about that "thingy" being part of our conversation. I *do* however, remember briefly mentioning that there was a *misinformation* about me having an autism spectrum disorder, which is referred to by some as *Asperger syndrome As-per-ger*. At absolutely no stage in our conversation *whatsoever* do I recall referencing a tall plant of the lily family with fine feathery foliage, cultivated for its edible shoots… otherwise known as *AS-PA-RA-GUS*!'

Tanya cupped her hands over her mouth in shock.

I sucked in more oxygen. 'It's OK. These things happen. If it's any personal consolation to myself, I was on the right track from the get-go. You're not an agent for the Deluney College bullying cartel. You're just unbelievably stupid.'

Cue a horrified look from Tanya. 'You… you think I'm stupid?'

'No.'

'That's what you said.'

'No, I didn't.'

'*Yes*, you did!'

'I didn't say that I *think* you're stupid, Tanya. I said *you're stupid*. It was an affirmation, not an assumption.'

'Are you for real?!' Aggression was starting to creep into her voice.

'Look, Tanya, you shouldn't take offence because stupidity isn't something you choose. It relies heavily on genetics and as you and I both know, you certainly didn't choose from between whose legs you got pushed out from, so no hard feelings, but I prefer that we don't speak any more. I find stupidity taxing.'

'What makes you think I'm stupid?'

A metaphorical boulevard suddenly stretched out in front of me.

'Oh, where to begin. No sense of orientation, slow to respond to questions, difficulty in grasping basic concepts such as my name – which for the umpteenth time is *Leon*, not Noel – incorrectly repeating a confidential piece of misinformation about me, which, through your own mental carelessness, has now been grossly deformed and broadcast throughout the entire school!'

She stepped forward and eyeballed me. 'You done?'

'Well, I could also mention the fact that—'

'Because *I'm* talking now!' she yelled. 'All those reasons you think I'm stupid? They're actually common for someone who's dyslexic – which I am. Thanks for pointing out all the stuff I struggle with all the time, it's great to know that you're just like all the others round here. For the record, I *know* sometimes kids think I'm stupid, but I *know I'm not* and to be honest, I couldn't give a toss what anyone else thinks. You, however, are a *total* loser and you're not even aware of it. So how stupid does that make you, then?!'

She pulled a long cardboard tube from her bag, flung it in my direction and stormed off down the corridor.

Goodness knows, she probably meant to go the other way.

9
Strange Encounters

I figured that P.E was as good a time as any to sneak off school. All I had to do was hide in a changing room until everyone had regrouped in the main hall and then shuffle out of the nearest emergency exit.

The question was, where to now?

Home seemed like the most obvious choice but not the most strategic. Caroline was working evening shifts all week, so she'd probably be waiting for me impatiently at the kitchen table, fizzing with questions about Tanya, and school, and the like. Avoiding the homestead, however, meant that I would shortly have to find food.

I fished around in my pockets and found 93p in loose change: the exact price of a 200-gram bar of ASDA Fruit & Nut, so I headed off in that direction.

Supermarkets are, for me, what fire is to a snowman. Bright lights, squeaky trolley wheels on even squeakier lino floors, sudden announcements on loudspeakers that lacerate your inner ears. Hell on earth. But needs must, at the end of the day.

As soon as I'd passed through the automatic doors, I

hunched my shoulders and kept my eyes low to the ground. This didn't make navigating around the labyrinth of aisles very easy and I ended up veering towards the deli counter.

'Three containers of sardine-wrapped olives please.'

Oh no.

It couldn't be.

No, seriously, this had to be a set-up for some low-budget reality TV series.

'Leon?'

'Caroline.'

'What are *you* doing here?'

Yes, it was Caroline, and it was me, reunited by total chance at the deli counter of ASDA Blackpool Superstore on Cherry Tree Road. I'd have run straight to the cash desk and bought a lotto ticket except I'm underage.

'More importantly Caroline, what are *you* doing here?' I said. 'Your weekly grocery shop is traditionally Saturday mornings between 10.15 and 11.35 a.m.'

'Yeah, but I'm getting fed up with them running out of what I'm looking for by the time the weekend rolls around.'

'Well, at least you can be sure that your sardine-wrapped olives will always be plentiful, even in the case of a nuclear holocaust,' I told her as she took the see-through plastic containers from the lady at the counter.

'Fling those in the trolley for me, would you, lovie?'

I looked into the trolley. It was already stockpiled with

cartons of milk, bunches of bananas and sacks of McCain crinkle-cut oven chips. Nothing out of the ordinary. Hang on…

'What are *these* doing in here?' I held up a family fun-size pack of pickled-onion-flavoured Monster Munch.

'What? Those? I'm going to buy them.'

'No, you're not.'

'Yes, I am.'

'Caroline, since when are *you* eating Monster Munch?'

'Dunno,' she said. 'One of the gang at work got me into them recently. They're really addictive!'

'These things are a bio-chemical hazard, Caroline, that's what they are. They smell of fermented bodily fluids. You can't buy them. Put them back.'

'Yes, I can.'

'*No*, you can't. We have a no-Monster-Munch-eating policy in the house.'

'No, we don't.'

'As of now, we do. It's just come into force.'

She snatched the bag out of my hands. 'Fine then, I'll just eat them while I finish the shopping; was feeling a bit peckish anyway.'

She opened the bag just inches from my face, and a rancid stench of three-day-old wee wafted up into my nostrils. It took all my inner strength not to gag aloud.

'Leon, shouldn't you be home right now? I left your dinner out on the counter for you.'

Panic.

Hurry up, brain, hurry up.

'I wanted something different.'

Caroline's eyes somersaulted. 'Something different? *You?* Leon John Crothers? Want something *different*? For *your dinner*?'

'Yes.'

'Like what?'

Words, brain, quickly. And make sure they're coherent.

'Ham.'

Brain, you *donkey*.

Caroline gave me a suspicious look as she put the Monster Munch back in the trolley.

'Ham? Seriously? There's always ham in the fridge at home, but you refuse to eat it. You've always said that eating ham from out of a packet is like chewing on a sweaty armpit.'

Brain, redeem yourself immediately, or so help me God…

'Parma ham. I was looking for Parma ham.'

'*Parma* ham? Where'd you get an idea like that?'

'I don't know, I just had a sudden craving.'

'For *Parma ham*?'

'Just why are women allowed to have food cravings and not men? When you were pregnant with me, nobody made a fuss about you tearing strips of wallpaper off the dining-room wall and spreading them on toast, but I get a posh Italian ham hankering and it becomes a national scandal!'

'All right, all right, calm down,' she said as she called back over the lady working on the counter.

'I'll take some Parma ham as well, please. Leon, how many slices do you want?'

'Twelve.'

'Twelve?! Have you seen the price?'

'Yes.'

'You'd better not make a habit of this, or I'll be through my monthly pay-packet in less than a week. Gosh, this new school seems to be having quite the effect on you… Parma ham… next thing you know you'll be asking me to wrap it round asparagus.'

Oh for…

'You just had to mention the a-word, didn't you? You couldn't have said "radishes" or "celery" or "pak choi", no, no, no, it just *had* to be asparagus!'

Caroline looked increasingly perplexed. 'Why do I get a sneaky feeling that you aren't telling me the full story here?'

Uh-oh. It was time to get out of this conversational Russian roulette as fast as possible.

'Better get going. If the school rings, tell them I'm off till next week, would you?'

'Whoa, whoa, whoa, hang on a minute. You've been in your new school one day and you want to take four days off?'

'Correction: I've been at school for one and a half days. I am requesting three and a half days' respite.'

'Respite?'

'Yes, Caroline, respite.'

'From what?'

Brain? Brain??

'From… from…'

Blank. Nothing. Nada. My brain was officially on strike.

Luckily, by way of some divine intervention, Caroline unknowingly came to my rescue.

'This is about what Dr Snot said, isn't it? Oh, I'm sorry. I should have twigged it sooner. You're clearly dealing with a lot right now.'

Hallelujah!

'If you say so, Caroline,' I said. 'So, you'll make sure to call the school? Do the necessary, etc.?'

The deli counter lady handed over a slim wax paper package with the scandalous price printed out below the barcode.

'Leon, I'm not OK with getting you signed off for the rest of the week. OK for tomorrow, but on Thursday, your bum had better be back in Deluney.'

'OK, fine, so long as you promise to include this afternoon in the deal as well.'

She pursed her lips and dragged them to one side of her mouth, indicating that I was pushing it a bit with my demands, but I knew she'd give in in the end.

'Well, I've almost finished the shopping. Stay with me and I'll bring us both home in the van.'

'I'd rather go home by myself, Caroline. There's nothing I

hate more than the sound of a loaded trolley screeching over chipped tarmac in the car park. You know that.'

'At least take the money for your ham, then.'

She rummaged in her slouchy denim handbag and passed me over a tenner.

I said goodbye and headed over to the self-service checkout, where I discreetly dumped the ham behind a stack of TV guides before exiting.

A rough wind hit me head on as I cut through the rows of parked cars in the car park, accompanied by spitting rain. My head was throbbing. Far too much strenuous mental activity for one day. By the time I'd managed to locate the bus stop, which, of course, had to be one of those bus stops without a shelter, my hoodie was nicely damp. That didn't bother me a great deal, though. I was more put off by a strange-looking person already waiting at the stop, dressed in a full-length beige protective hazard suit and matching helmet. Even though I couldn't see the wearer's face, which was well camouflaged behind the helmet's sheet of netting, I knew I was being watched. But the weirdest detail is yet to come: my ham parcel was being held hostage between a pair of black gloves.

Who was this freak?

Then, out of nowhere, it spoke.

'Hello, Leon. I'm Lawrence. Lawrence, your classmate.'

He held out the ham package towards me.

'You forgot this at ASDA. Don't worry, I paid for it. We all can forget our money at the most inconvenient of times.'

I was half-tempted to put this Lawrence lad in his place by telling him that I'd left the ham at the checkout on purpose, but felt it was better to keep dialogue to a strict minimum. For all I knew, he was testing out that hazmat suit because he was plotting to pump noxious gases through Deluney's vent system and poison us all to death.

'We sit nearest each other in geography Leon. Did you know that we sit nearest each other in geography, Leon? Do you like geography, Leon?'

The bus *needed* to come. I really wasn't in the mood for small talk, or social niceties, and I certainly wasn't in the mood for gifted meat of any kind.

'You must be feeling terrible about the whole asparagus misunderstanding, Leon,' he continued. 'I can help you with that. That's why I followed you here.'

Creepy. Like serial-killer creepy.

'We're the same, you and I.'

OK, there was no way I could stay quiet after a comment like that.

'The same? Us two? Far from it,' I shot back. 'For one thing, I don't go around wearing ridiculous sci-fi jumpsuits and stalk my classmates to supermarkets where I pick up the bill for their unpurchased cold cuts.'

He suddenly stood up, walked right up close to me and took

off his helmet. His skin was so pale it was almost translucent, and heavily marked by freckles. A wispy blonde fringe clung to the sides of his forehead like a frayed curtain.

He spoke with a toothy grin.

'This is a bee-keeping suit. I wear it when it rains. It's a great way of staying toasty and dry outdoors. Bee-keeping suits are handy things. I've got three others at home. I'm a beekeeper in my spare time. *Apis mellifera*. That's the Latin name for the domesticated western honeybee. It's the only species of honeybee native to the United Kingdom. Did you know that the number of managed honeybee colonies in the UK fell by fifty-three per cent between 1985 and 2005? That's an urgent bee fact. I've got *lots* of urgent bee facts, Leon. Did you know that one third of the UK's bee population has disappeared over the past decade? Did you know that twenty-four per cent of Europe's bumblebees are currently threatened with extinction? Did you know that if bees disappeared off the face of the earth, man would have only *four years to live*? That's why I keep bees in the field behind where I live: Bethany Crescent. Number twelve. Tanya lives there too. Number sixty-four. Do you know Tanya Asher? From our class? She's the girl who mispronounced your Asperger's diagnosis when she was speaking to Claire Abrahams in P.E on Monday afternoon. Do you know that I have Asperger's just like you, Leon? It's like we're the same species. So, you can count on me as a friend. Just like the bees, we must stay strong in the face of adversity.

We Aspies must stick together! That's a funny bee joke for you – stick together – bees – honey. Did you get the joke, Leon?'

'TAXI!'

A passing black cab pulled up beside us and I piled my sopping wet self into the back seat before he even had a chance to catch his breath.

10
Caroline's Idea of Fun

Everything you need to know about where I live (with Caroline):

1. We live in a poky, 2-bedroom detached bungalow, 2km east of Blackpool
2. Caroline began renting the bungalow just before I was born
3. When she first moved into the bungalow, the bathroom was fully carpeted
4. Our bathroom is still fully carpeted
5. Caroline avoids household chores that involve pushing things in a repetitive manner (hoovering, lawnmowing, mopping, sweeping, ironing, etc.)
6. I avoid household chores that involve irritating noises (hoovering, lawnmowing, mopping, sweeping, ironing, etc.)
7. The grass in our back garden is very high

If you're actually paying attention to what you're reading, then you'll remember that on the first page of Chapter 2, I told you that I don't like surprises. Caroline, on the other hand, is quite partial to the thrill of the unexpected (hence the illegitimate child, one can presume). So, it shouldn't come as a shock to you that we tend to clash on the subject, especially as Caroline's surprises are often badly timed.

Today's was no exception.

Not one for lazing around mid-week, I was up, showered, fed, watered and back in pyjamas before 9 a.m. I had a busy school-free Wednesday ahead of me, propped up by a demanding to-do list that I'd scrawled on the back of my hand in black biro:

1. Don't think about Glen
2. Don't think about Tanya
3. Don't think about asparagus

Shrewd Caroline, as always, was going to obliterate all that.

She chose the perfect moment to ambush me – when I was pushing out a Snickers on the loo – and therefore at my most vulnerable.

'Leon, when you're finished in there, could you pop outside and help me get the lawnmower out of the shed?'

Why the lawnmower? Why on a chilly, overcast morning when rain was due? Why with such enthusiasm? Why bother at all?

In any other situation, I would have spitfired these

questions back at her in response, but, as Caroline knew fully well, I *cannot* engage in conversation when emptying my bowels. There needs to be silence. Minimum distraction, maximum concentration.

'OK, fine.'

Fourteen minutes later, I emerged from the now heavily scented bathroom, and wandered sluggishly out the back door, which was rattling on its hinges from the intense vibrations coming from the far end of the garden. A truck with an enormous flatbed trailer was backing into our large grassy plot from a neighbouring field.

I stood in the doorway and watched a couple of burly workmen separate the trailer from the truck. One of them blew a kiss to Caroline but she didn't seem to notice. She was far too busy dancing around me, gesticulating like a possessed puppet, singing, 'Welcome to the house of fun, na na na na na, welcome to the house of fun!'

That's exactly what it was: a funhouse. A genuine fairground funhouse had just been reversed into our back garden.

Caroline managed to come out of her trance just in time to wave goodbye to the driver.

'Cheers, Jim, you're one in a gazillion!'

'Enjoy, lass!' he shouted back.

The truck disappeared down the road with a honk of its horn, leaving just the three of us: me, Caroline and the metallic monstrosity.

'Well? What do you think??' she squealed.

I thought for a moment.

'To be honest, Caroline, I think that turning our oversized and overgrown back garden into a scrapyard isn't a bad idea at all. It would generate some extra income when needed.'

Her face dropped. 'Leon, I'm not turning our back garden into a scrapyard.'

'Then why is that rusty, knackered-looking eyesore sitting twenty-five metres from our house?'

'It's for you, silly billy!'

'My name's not Billy, it's—'

'D'you know that the boys at work were going to turf this beauty? The *minute* they told me it was on its way to the tip, I said I'd take it off their hands. I thought it would be the perfect place for you to—'

'What? Play? Oh, how thoughtful, Caroline. It's true that I've been really struggling to fit into my plastic turtle sandpit as of late.'

Caroline was now beginning to get flustered; the red blotches on her neck were always a dead giveaway.

'Well, not *play*, obviously. I was thinking it could make a cool hangout place for you and your friends.'

My eyes narrowed. 'Based on what you *just* said, Caroline, please take note of the following points. One: "thinking" clearly isn't one of your strengths. Two: your personal definition of "cool" visibly doesn't correspond with that of my peers. Three:

your vision that I may one day make a friendly connection with someone that is meaningful enough to invite them to visit this banjaxed whacky shack is completely warped. Four: taking into account my abysmal coordination skills and sporting endurance, for you to even think that I would want to "hang out" of *any* structure whatsoever shows that you barely know me at all.'

I charged back into the house, grabbing a carton of milk from the fridge before holing myself up in my room for the rest of the morning.

Caroline let me be. When I ventured out of my bedroom around midday, I saw that she'd gone to the trouble of leaving my dinner on a tray outside my door with a note saying:

Sorry – If you need help with your to-do list, I'm here.

Caroline's good like that.

11

Conversations with the Boogerman

'Leon John Crothers to see Dr Snot.'

The receptionist gave me the once-over through her red plastic reading glasses.

'Have you got an appointment?'

'Yes.'

'Wednesday the fifth? 2 p.m.? Don't seem to have you down here.'

'Of course you don't. I haven't got an appointment.'

'But you just said—'

'I know what I just said, no need to repeat it. I was just proving a point to myself that receptionists are nothing but—'

'But *what*?' she snarled back.

Perhaps it was time to try a more softly-softly approach.

'I want to speak to Dr Snot. *Now.*'

'You can't without an appointment.'

'But I want to speak to him.'

'Not without an appointment. Sorry I can't be of any more help,' she smarmed.

'OK, fine,' I said as I crossed the waiting room to Dr Snot's office and opened the door.

The doc was sitting in his leather easy chair, polishing off a pasty.

'Leon! What a surprise! Were we supposed to be meeting today?'

The receptionist started squawking like a deranged parrot from the desk.

'I'll be quick, Doc,' I assured him. 'I've got other important things to do today. Also, your heavy nicotine addiction, nestled snugly in the fibres of your clothes, wreaks havoc with my nostrils.'

'I see,' replied the doc and gestured reassuringly to his receptionist, as he closed the door.

'In fact, that's why I've dropped by,' I explained. 'To give you these.'

I tossed a clear plastic bag onto the doc's desk.

The doc examined the bag up close. 'Black jelly beans, eh?'

'When Ronald Reagan ran for Governor of California in 1966, he began eating Goelitz Mini Jelly Beans, known today as Jelly Belly beans, as part of a successful attempt to give up pipe smoking. In 1981, when Reagan was elected President of the United States, three and a half tons of red, white and blue Jelly Belly jelly beans were shipped to Washington, DC for the inauguration festivities. Herman Goelitz Candy Company provided the White House with Jelly Belly jelly beans for all eight years of Reagan's presidency. The company even received official government authorisation to develop a Jelly Belly jelly-bean jar with the presidential seal on it.'

'Very interesting, Leon. And I suppose the choice of the black-coloured jelly bean is an ode to my smoke-ravaged insides. Am I right?'

'No. President Reagan's favourite jelly-bean flavour was liquorice. It's just a pleasant coincidence.'

'Liquorice? Is that so?' mused the doc. 'Well, thank you for the thoughtful gesture, Leon. I'll be sure to let you know how I get on.'

We then sat in silence. Dr Snot didn't seem fazed by the absence of words. He just smiled back at me and formed a steeple shape with his fingers against his nose.

Eventually he said, 'Can I suppose that hand-delivering these jelly beans wasn't the only reason that you've come to see me today?'

'It's more or less a free country – suppose away.'

'Tell you what. I'm going to let you do the talking from now on.'

'I think if you were to tally the verbal word count since I've arrived in your office, Doc, you'd realise that I've largely dominated in the conversation stakes.'

Silence.

True to his word, the doc was giving nothing back. Now he wasn't even looking at me any more, but at the fresh mustard stain on his trouser leg instead.

Well, here goes nothing.

'Apparently I'm incapable of knowing when I'm being a loser. Does that mean I'm stupid?'

The doc's eyebrows shot up. '*That's* a loaded question. Where did you come up with that one?'

'A girl in my new, new, new, new, new, new, new school said that. She's nice enough, but she suffers from crippling stupidity disease – clearly not her fault, chromosomes, etc. You know, such is life.'

'A stupidity disease?'

'Yes. Dyslexia, it's called. She seems completely fine with it, though. The fact that she's so stupid means she's probably living in some blissful state of denial.'

'Well, I certainly wouldn't label dyslexia as a stupidity disease,' the doc cautioned, sitting up broadly in his chair. 'Dyslexia is a neurological learning disability. In other words, if someone has dyslexia, his or her brain is simply wired to handle information differently. People with dyslexia might take a bit longer to process new information. They can also find reading, writing or spelling more difficult. But by the sheer nature of their condition, dyslexics have to use their cognitive creativity to find different ways to get things done. In fact, I was recently reading a paper on the subject from a professor at a leading American university who described dyslexia as the disorder of the geniuses.'

My mouth sprang open. 'Disorder of the geniuses?! A girl who doesn't know that we're living on Planet Earth has a genius disorder?'

'Did she really say that?'

'Yes. During our first conversation, which took place beside the vending machine in the west wing of Deluney College, she said, and I quote, "Eh, what planet are we on?", to which I responded the obvious. Then seconds after, she followed up with: "You sure we're on Planet Earth?"'

The doc stroked his bulbous chin. 'Hmm… are you sure she wasn't being ironic?'

'Ironic?'

'Irony: the use of words to express something other than and especially the opposite of their literal meaning. Do you know that interpreting irony is something that many people with autism spectrum disorders struggle with? Idioms too.'

'Doc, I *don't* have an autism spectrum disorder. I don't even have nits.'

'Then explain this to me, Leon: why did you hop out of my office after our first meeting?'

'Because Caroline said, "Leon, hop to it."'

'Do you know that "hop to it" is an idiom that means to move quickly? People with ASDs often have difficulty with phrases that are not literal, such as idioms. An idiom is a word or phrase that means something different from its literal meaning. "Break a leg", for example, is an idiom for "good luck".'

The doc spun his chair round to the messy shelves behind him and dragged a sausage-shaped finger along a row of book spines.

'Ah! Here's a book for you on the subject. A token gift of gratitude for the jelly beans.'

I stared down at the book on his desk. 'So, turns out there might be something wrong with me after all, Doc.'

The doc smiled and rested his folded arms on his desk. 'From what I can see, Leon, the only thing wrong with you is that you're looking at all of this from the *wrong* perspective. Nobody is saying that any of this is easy and I'm sure your friend—'

'She's not my friend—'

'Well, I'm sure this girl you mentioned has many challenges with her dyslexia too, but it sounds as though she has embraced her condition and turned it into a noteworthy strength. That's very courageous of her. She might well be a strong ally for you in school going forward.'

'She gave me this the other day,' I said, taking out the cardboard tube from my rucksack.

'What is it?' asked the doc.

'Don't know. I haven't opened it yet.'

'Would you like me to?'

'Go ahead. I figure that if it's a coded death threat or something, you'd have the medical sway to have her admitted.'

I handed over the tube. The doc removed the white, disc-shaped lid and pulled out a large sheet of paper. Then he leant back in his chair and unrolled it in front of his eyes.

'Oh my!'

Without thinking, I lunged across the desk and snatched the sheet of paper from his hands.

My eyes rapidly scanned the image from side to side. I was so taken aback that a rogue smile escaped from the corners of my mouth. It was a drawing of, well, this:

From what seemed like a far distance, I could hear the doc chuckling to himself.

'What did I tell you, eh? The disorder of the geniuses, my boy!'

With my eyes still transfixed on the drawing, I stood up and manoeuvred my way blindly out of Dr Snot's office. The doc had surely noticed that I'd left his book behind, but he didn't call after me to come back and get it.

He knew better than to spoil the moment.

12
Dyslexics are Teople Poo

Just so we're clear, this isn't the sort of thing I usually do. For one thing, I've never shown up on someone's doorstep unannounced. I've never had a reason to show up on anyone's doorstep, full stop.

I hadn't planned to track down Tanya's address for fear of being labelled a juvenile stalker. But seeing as how Lawrence had treated me to a full helping of verbal diarrhoea during our paranormal encounter, when this chunk of information spewed out, I decided to make use of it.

Turns out Tanya's address, Bethany Crescent, is just six bus stops from my bungalow. There really isn't much to say about the place: a standard cluster of horizontal grey cinderblocks with a load of noisy seagulls and satellite dishes on the roofs.

When I rang the doorbell at number sixty-four later that afternoon, Tanya answered. She was wearing an oversized blue shirt that was covered in neon paint. There were splodges on her face and her Afro was stuffed into a large silk headscarf.

'What are you doing?' I asked.

'Eh, I think *I* should be asking that question,' she replied. 'That and how the hell did you find out where I live? Are you like stalking me or what?'

'No. Lawrence, the oddball in our class, mentioned that you guys were both quote unquote neighbours.'

'Why's he telling people that?' she snapped. 'I barely ever see him round here. Boy's a complete weirdo. All he does is blab on about insects.'

'Bees.'

'Whatever. He should mind his own business. What you want?'

Cue the inevitable awkward silence.

To be fair, I had started pondering that question on the bus ride over. It was obvious that Tanya was going to ask me why I wanted to see her, and I had planned to be at least a little bit prepared. But then I got distracted by a large piece of luminous pink gum that was stuck to the back of the seat in front of me and spent the rest of the bus journey trying to work out if it was a Hubba Bubba, Bazooka or Bubbaloo. Now I was paying for it.

When she started looking down at her watch, I knew I had to act fast.

'This is for you.'

I handed over a small, glass cylinder.

She shook it and gave me an intimidating look.

'Sprinkles? You looking for me to bake you a Happy Loser

Day cake or something?'

Charming.

'They're not sprinkles… they're *fancy* sprinkles.'

'Oh, they're *fancy*, are they? If you say so…'

'Uh, you've got it all wrong! Fancy Sprinkles is the name of a sprinkle-manufacturing company based in Los Angeles. Seriously, we're talking the Bugatti Centodieci of sprinkles.'

She still seemed miffed. Hmm… perhaps she had a limited knowledge of luxury automobiles.

'Apparently, Beyoncé's a fan,' I said.

Total. Unapologetic. Lie.

Nothing. Not so much as a blink.

'That sprinkle mix is in fact a limited-edition mix called Freak Show, which the company brought out this year for Halloween, which by the way is *not* meant to cause offence, it's simply the name they gave to their seasonal product offering, it says so right there on the packaging.'

She looked back down at the cylinder. 'So, it's a gift, then, is it?'

My feet shuffled clumsily on the tatty welcome mat. 'Well, you know, one gifted tube deserves another and all that.'

'And all that?'

She really was making this *unbelievably* hard.

'Can I come in?'

'Why?'

'I need to use the loo.'

Tanya gave me another once-over with her eyes, before she let out a weighty sigh and stepped back from the door. 'Down the hall, second door on the right.'

'Is that the left right or the right right?'

'The right right,' she replied through gritted teeth.

'The right right. Right so.'

Fourteen minutes later, I came out of the bathroom, feeling considerably lighter, and went to find Tanya. She'd gone back to her bedroom. I glanced through the half-open door. There were drawings *everywhere*. Her wardrobe doors and desk were covered in multi-coloured doodles and every inch of wall space was covered up with sketches, from flowers to jellyfish to lava-belching volcanoes.

Tanya was sitting cross-legged on the floor, adding the finishing touches to a dramatic painting of some mythical creature with multiple heads.

'I'm kind of in the middle of something,' she said. 'You can let yourself out.'

'Can I stay?'

'No.'

'Why?'

'Because.'

'Why?'

'*Because.*'

'Why?'

She slammed her paintbrush down onto her wooden

palette, sending purple dollops of paint flying. 'Because you're a loser! You might be a loser with "fancy sprinkles", but let's be clear about one thing, yeah? You're a loser!'

'But—'

She jumped to her feet. '*Sorry* was all you had to say. "Tanya, *I'm sorry*." But no, you couldn't do that, could ya? Because that would mean admitting that you're a loser, which, as we both know already, is like, *mission impossible*.'

Then, as quickly as she'd stood up, she slumped back down onto the carpet and carried on painting.

Frustration, disappointment.

I backed out of her room and walked slowly down the hall to the living room, before stopping at the front door.

Frustration, anger, disappointment, upset.

Why couldn't I have been better prepared?

Hubba Bubba. It was definitely Hubba Bubba. No question.

I reached for the door handle.

Panic. Frustration.

I really didn't like what was happening. Worse than that, I hated feeling like I couldn't do something to make things better.

'Just so you know,' I called back over my shoulder. 'I was never planning to say sorry. I felt that if I said sorry, you'd expect me to not to behave the way that I did, ever again. The truth is, I may well have a brain condition that doesn't make social interaction easy. In fact, most of the time I get things very, very wrong. So that means that I'm likely to always say inappropriate things and behave differently to what is seen as "the norm". Hopefully in the future I can try and make less of them, but facts are facts, my brain is wired in a certain way and I just have to deal with that. So, if "sorry" is the word you really need to hear, then I'm sorry. And also, I think you should know that I don't think you're stupid. You're not stupid at all. You have serious talent.'

'I know.'

My skeleton almost jumped out of my skin. Tanya had crept down the hallway and was now standing right behind me.

'Are you insane?! You just scared the Snickers out of me. No seriously, I was a nanosecond away from pebble-dashing your living-room floor.'

'You trying to tell me that after all that time in my bog, you still got unfinished business?'

'My bowels go into overdrive when I'm feeling under pressure. Forces beyond my control.'

She smirked and the tension eased. 'For the record, whatever you've got, I'm OK with it. You've got a worse deal. *You're* the one who has to put up with me calling you Noel most of the time.'

'I read online that difficulty with letter sequencing when reading is common for those with dyslexia.'

'You got rat tight!' Tanya joked.

It was a funny joke, but I didn't let my face show it. Still too risky.

'D'you know, I actually thought that you were calling me Noel because you thought I looked like Noel Gallagher?'

'Noel Gallagher? From Oasis? Ha! Well, you do have the same couldn't-give-a-toss haircut.' She laughed.

'You've heard of Noel Gallagher?'

'Eh, yeah, like everybody else on Planet Earth.'

So, she *does* understand what planet we're on.

'He's dyslexic too, you know.'

My eyes widened. 'Noel Gallagher is dyslexic? *Noel Gallagher? Seriously?* Now you mention it, he *is* a musical, lyrical and philosophical genius and you know what they say: dyslexia is the disorder of the geniuses.'

'Matt Damon is dyslexic as well. Then there's Tom Cruise, Jennifer Aniston, Orlando Bloom, Muhammad Ali, Richard Branson, Keira Knightly.'

'Some luck,' I huffed. 'The autism hall of fame is a lot less glamourous. Just a mass murderer, a heretic, an abuser and a wig-wearing harpsicord player.'

'Aren't there rumours on the internet that Tim Burton has the same thing you have?'

'Tim Burton's autistic? Oh, God. Not the man who dug up Willy Wonka's well-buried cinematic corpse in 2005 and paraded it around the box office for an easy buck.'

'What?'

'It's a long story, never mind.'

'Are you bad-mouthing Tim Burton? Are you *seriously* dissing the creator of Jack Skeleton—'

'Correction: Jack Skellington.'

'Yeah, whatever. He, like, invented *The Nightmare Before Christmas*, and *Frankenweenie*, and *Edward Scissorhands*.'

'OK, fair dues, *Edward Scissorhands* is a pretty decent film.'

'Pretty decent, are you bonkers?!' Tanya wailed. 'It's like the best movie ever! That and *Beetlejuice*. I've got all Tim Burton's films. You wanna stay and watch some?'

Did she… did she just ask me to not go away?

'OK, fine.'

Tanya told me to pick a spot on the sofa while she went back to her room to get changed. My heart bounced around my ribcage as I wiped the warm moisture on my palms down the front of my jeans. Luckily, I'd brought a large bag of jazzies with me, on the very slim off-chance that I was invited to overstay my welcome.

13
Further Unpleasantness

You wouldn't believe me if I told you, but today for the first time in my life, I was *excited* to go to school. Not to chum about with my uniformed peers or listen to yet another below-average educator drone on about trivial facts that will in no way contribute to my success or failure in adulthood. I was excited because, after yesterday's Tim Burton movie marathon, Tanya had asked me what the creepiest sweets I'd ever eaten were. I said that I'd think about it and tell her the next day during our dinner break and she said 'Cool.' She even asked me for my mobile number, 'in case of'.

I'd been up half the night drafting the shortlist, which I perfected during the morning lessons.

Here's the final version:

The Creepiest Sweets I've Ever Eaten
1. Pulse candy from India — a round, mango-flavoured hard candy with a sulphur (i.e. rotten egg) tasting powder inside.
2. Jane-Jane Tasty Tuna Tidbits from China — honey-

coloured hard candy drops that taste like tuna fish...
on purpose.

3. Thanksgiving gumballs from Washington, USA –
featuring turkey, cranberry sauce and pumpkin pie. Eat
all three at once for a complete holiday feast.

4. Musk sticks from Australia – hard candy sticks that taste
like a bottle of grandad's cologne.

5. Hose Nose candy from San Diego, USA – A plastic
nose-shaped dispenser that holds candy slime. Let
the slime drip from the nose onto your tongue for a
(delicious?) green apple snack.

6. Durian candy from Singapore – dried fruit candy that
smells like turpentine and sweaty gym socks. Durian
fruit itself is in fact banned from consumption in
transport systems, hospitals and hotels across many
parts of South-East Asia.

7. Cheese pizza chocolate from Japan – yup. A chocolate
bar with a cheese-pizza-flavoured mousse filling.

'Grab us a seat in the canteen, will ya?' Tanya said just as the
bell rang at the end of history class. 'Gotta swing by the loo.'

'As if this place wasn't shambolic enough.' I guffawed.
'Why would they go and install a swing beside the toilets?'

Tanya rolled her eyes and blew a stream of air out of her
mouth. 'I have to *go* to the loo, that better?'

'Well, it's certainly more reassuring,' I replied as I stopped at my locker to grab my knife and fork.

The canteen was packed when I arrived. Junk-food Friday certainly attracted the crowds. I queued for two portions of burger and chips; one for Tanya and one for me to pretend play with. I figured bringing a banana-themed meal from home would have just led unwanted attention from troublemakers. Besides, filling my stomach could wait – especially when there was a golden opportunity to discuss cheese-pizza-flavoured chocolate and the like.

I had just found a spot for us at the end of a long table when I was set upon.

'All right, mate?'

Glen was hovering over my seat, backed by a couple of lads who looked like they had a court appearance pending.

'Just wanted to a-po-lo-gise for the whole name-callin' thing. Yer little friend over there came to see me yes-ta-day to put things right.'

He cocked a thumb over his shoulder towards Lawrence, who was sitting alone on a chair beside the entrance to the canteen, fiddling with the latch on his lunchbox.

I stood up to leave, but two hands the size of oven mitts appeared from overhead and pushed me back down.

'Where you off to?' Glen said with a smirk as he sat down in what was supposed to be Tanya's seat. His two goons stayed directly behind me. 'What you got there? Two burgers? Greedy, greedy...' He went to pick up the burger on Tanya's plate.

'*Don't…*' I threatened, making a grab for the tray, but the mitts held me back.

'Getting tetchy now, are ya? Looks like me and the lads are disturbin' yer dinner. We'll let you get on wiv it, so.'

Suddenly, I was dragged to my feet, and my tray was slid down onto the bench, directly underneath me.

Panic. Fear. Rage. Helplessness.

'Enjoy your food, *ass-burger*.'

Then it came.

Splat.

They slammed me back down onto the bench. Meat, ketchup, mayo, cheese, tomato, lettuce, gherkin squirted out from my trousers in all directions.

Fits of laughter rang out around the hall.

I made a break for it, pushing through the groups of hysterically laughing faces and pointing fingers.

'ASSBURGER! ASSBURGER! ASSBURGER! ASSBURGER!'

The chants followed me down the main corridor, then right and then left, until I reached the disabled toilets and barricaded myself inside.

Rage. Confusion. Embarrassment. Rage. Confusion. Embarrassment…

There was a knock on the door.

'Leon? It's Lawrence. Are you in there?'

I swung open the door and pulled Lawrence inside by his shirt collar.

'Hi, friend. What was all that commotion in the canteen just now? Why do you smell like meat? Did you pick a fight with Glen? Don't tell me I need to go and talk to him *again*?'

I pushed my chest up close to his and hissed out instructions between the gaps in my teeth. 'Tell me exactly what you said to Glen.'

He looked back at me with round, innocent eyes. 'Well, I think the—'

'Not what you *think*… tell me what you *said*.'

After a brief pause, he got himself into position and made beak shapes with his hands. 'OK. Here's *exactly* what happened: "Hi, Glen." "Bugger off." "Glen, I have to talk to you about the new chap in our class, Leon—" "You deaf? *Bugger off*—" "Glen, there's something important about Leon that you should know. You see, Leon has an autism spectrum disorder often referred to as Asperger syndrome, so—" "Get to the point, ya little snitch!" "The thing is, Tanya actually mispronounced Leon's condition when she was speaking to Claire in P.E the other day, who spoke to Sandra, who spoke to Kevin, who—" "*So?!*" "So maybe you could tell everyone to stop calling Leon 'asparagus'? Because, well, he's not an asparagus, is he? No. He's a human being, just like the rest of us. This has all been just one huge misunderstanding. Long words can be tricky things. I find that they're always easier to say if they're broken down into smaller words. For example, As-per-ger's could be broken down into 'ass' and 'burger'.

Then all you do is replace the 'b' in 'burger' with a 'p'. Ass-burger… Ass-pur-ger."'

I grabbed the back of my head with my hands and dragged my fingers down through my hair.

'*Ass-burger*…? You told Glen Jenkins to stop calling me 'asparagus', and proposed '*ass-burger*' as a suitable alternative?'

Lawrence dropped his hand-puppets. 'Eh, I guess, well, when you put it like that—'

Rage. Incandescent rage.

My foot slammed into the small metal bin beside the sink, sending it rolling around the tiles. Lawrence muffled his ears with his hands.

'How can you be so stupid?! Do you know that having imbeciles like *you* living and breathing on this planet puts into jeopardy the progress and wellbeing of the entire human race? Specimens like you who are so ignorant, so careless, so terrifyingly out of touch with the real world, should be wiped out at the youngest age so that society doesn't have to pay the financial and humanitarian price to clean up the trail of destruction that you leave in your wake!'

I flung open the bathroom door, almost bulldozing into Tanya, who was standing just behind it, and sped off.

She ran down the corridor after me. 'Noel, wait! I've been looking for you everywhere! Noel! Slow down! Wait!'

Too late. I was gone.

And I was never coming back.

14
The Attack

Funny things, car crashes.

Now, before you start sounding the 'attitude problem' alarm, just hear me out, OK?

In principle, car crashes aren't funny, unless they involve test dummies or evil villains. Even *I* know that.

What is funny is how people react to a car crash when they drive past one, on the motorway for example.

Car crashes bring out the gawker in us all. We can't stop ourselves from pressing our faces up against the windows and ogling the wreckage as soon as it comes into sight. This inevitably causes a huge backlog of annoyed drivers who'll beep and swear but will repeat the same slow-down-and-stare ritual when their turn comes.

Just before you pass by the scene of a crash, there's always a sudden rush of anticipation. How many mangled vehicles will there be? Will there be airbags mushrooming up out of a shattered windscreen? A bumper pleated up like an accordion? Will there be a person screaming their lungs out as the emergency services attempt to cut them out of their seat? Will there be blood and bits of intestines strewn across the road? Will there be victims? Will there be survivors?

But here's the most important question: if you *do* see something terrible, do you turn away, or do you keep looking?

OK, I'm getting a bit ahead of myself here, but keep what I said in mind – you'll see why in a bit.

Picking back up from where we left off, I'd just ditched Deluney on foot, vowing never to return. I can't remember much about the walk home, except that I smelt very greasy. It's a bit of a blur, to be honest.

Back in the bungalow, Caroline was sitting on the living-room sofa in her moulting woolly dressing-gown, watching *The Chase* with the volume up way too loud.

'What's going on?' she gasped in surprise.

'The washing machine,' I answered as I stripped down to my boxers right there in front of her.

'How'd you manage that one, then? Slip on a banana peel?' She was giggling now.

'Not funny, Caroline,' I replied curtly. 'Not funny in the slightest.'

'Ah, come on, I was only kidding. Do you want me to fetch you a change of clothes so that you can get back to school before the – '

'No thanks, Caroline.'

I went to the bathroom for a much-needed wee and an unexpected poo. Then I showered and washed my hair – two shampoos, one conditioner. When I'd finished in the shower, a wide ray of sunshine was beaming through the bathroom skylight, so I decided for forgo the traditional towel-dry and lay down on the carpeted floor instead. The dusty fibres felt coarse and prickly against my skin, but I didn't mind; the warm sun more than made up for it.

I closed my eyes and exhaled slowly.

Where to from here?

The answer was a no-brainer: bed. After a short sunbathing stint, I willed myself up from the bathroom carpet, wandered stark naked down the hallway and locked myself in my room. Just as I was on the point of dozing off, Caroline tapped on the door.

'Are you heading back to school, then?'

'No, Caroline.'

'But they'll be wondering where you are.'

'I highly doubt that, Caroline.'

For a moment, there was perfect silence. I didn't expect it to last long, though. Caroline was still behind the door; I could smell her almond-scented hand cream.

Eventually she said, 'Lovie, is there something you're not telling me?'

'Yes.'

'Well, when are you going to tell me the thing you're not telling me?'

She waited a few minutes for a response, but when none

came, she took the hint and shuffled off.

I slept all afternoon until teatime, when I took in my plate of pizza and chips from outside my door. Caroline had already left for her evening work shift, but she'd left a note on my tray, saying:

Told school you were sick. Feel better soon.

From there, it was a quick trip to the bathroom for a teeth-brush and a tinkle, then back to bed for another marathon sleep.

The starlings in our gutter woke me early the next morning, with their annoying hunger cheeps. By early, I mean 7 a.m., so yes, proper early for a sick day.

I'd had an agitated night's sleep, full of strange dreams that seemed to tiptoe in and out of reality. Worse still, my subconscious was interrupted a number of times by what seemed like a giant invisible bee buzzing right beside my ear.

I began searching for my phone between the pleats of bobbled cotton. When I finally found it, I saw five missed calls from Tanya from the night before.

She'd also sent a text:

CALLL IN SERIUS TROUBLE

Tanya. Tanya's in trouble. Tanya's in serious trouble.

I vaulted out of bed, grabbed a hoodie off my chest of

drawers and scrambled to dress myself.

Tanya. Tanya's in trouble. Tanya's in serious trouble.

Bus times couldn't be trusted this early in the morning, so I dragged Caroline's high nelly bicycle out of the porch and pedalled clumsily down the dimly lit street, then out onto the main road and on towards Bethany Crescent.

Tanya. Tanya's in trouble. Tanya's in serious trouble.

I couldn't believe it when I saw Tanya crossing the road in front of her flat at the very same moment I skidded up onto the kerb. As I leapt off the saddle, the bike toppled over, and I got my legs tangled in the pedals and ended up in a heap at her shoes.

'Eh, all right, Noel?' she said through the tail end of a yawn.

'Who? What? When? Where? Why?' I puffed, half out of breath as I staggered to my feet.

'Ya what?'

'Who? What? Where? When? Why? *Quickly!*'

'Tanya Asher, walking, bus stop, right now, going to school.'

'Time for joking, is it?'

'Noel, it's too early for this. I'm half asleep. What you doing outside my place at this hour, anyway?'

'What happened? Tell me what happened to you! How am I supposed to help you if you don't tell me what happened?!'

I turned around Tanya in a circle, looking for missing limbs, a foot in a bear trap, a family of snakes nesting in her giant pom-pom.

'What you playing at, Noel?! *Nothing*'s happened to me! Stop acting mental!'

'Then why did you send me a message last night saying you were in serious trouble?'

'No, I didn't.'

'Yes, you did!'

'No.'

'Yes!'

'No.'

I pulled out my phone and flashed the bright screen up under her eyes.

CALLL IN SERIUS TROUBLE

'There! That enough proof for you?' I wheezed.

'Eh, yeah, that I'm right and you're wrong,' she threw back at me.

'What?!'

'Read it yourself. It says, *Call. L in serious trouble*. As in, *Lawrence is in serious trouble*.'

'No, it doesn't!'

'Well, that's what I meant.'

I felt the blood slowly drain from my face as I stumbled to sit down on the kerb. 'Once again, Tanya, your genius disorder has been a catalyst for disaster. All this forced exercise has most likely caused irreparable damage to my pulmonary arteries.'

She slung herself down beside me. 'Sorry. My bad.'

The number 11 bus whirred past us, lit up like an arcade game.

'You going to run after it?' I asked. 'With a bit of leg effort, you'd probably manage it.'

'Nah, we can catch the next one when you've your energy back.'

'I'm not going to school, Tanya. But judging by that message of yours, I highly recommend that *you* get to school as fast is as humanly possible...'

She slapped me round the back of the head, then began searching through her bag. 'Fancy a bit of Rice Krispies Square?'

'Is that a genuine question, Tanya? In that case, no, I'd rather lick a cactus. You really shouldn't be stuffing your face with those fake breakfast foods.'

I made a grab for the foiled package, but she demonstrated impressive hand-eye coordination skills.

'*Nobody* takes my food away from me. *Ever.* Got it?'

The sticky puffed rice rectangle then disappeared into her mouth, all in one go. I was amazed at how little chewing it took for the thing to slide down her oesophagus.

'So, you really don't care about what happened to Lawrence, then?' she asked me.

'Lawrence? What about Lawrence?'

'That he's been in serious trouble.'

'Not in the slightest. Have you already forgotten the scale

of the chaos his meddling landed me in? Literally? I should be howling at the moon in gratitude that justice has been served.'

There was a sudden drop in conversation.

Tanya was staring blankly into the morning mist, shaking her head slowly from side to side.

'Oh, no need for dramatics, Tanya,' I said. '*What?* What happened to the little pleb? Did someone use honey to glue his copy books together?'

She continued to stare off into nowhere as she spoke. 'Someone from the flats found Lawrence in the field round the back of the estate yesterday evening. He was in a really bad way. They managed to get him talking and wanted to call for help, but he just begged to be brought home to his mum—'

'Blah, blah, blah... so, he got lost in the shrubs. What's the big deal? That's not even justice, Tanya. That's forgetfulness.'

She gave me a stone-faced look. 'You're gonna feel a right idiot in a few minutes.'

'Is *that* how long you plan to ramble on for?' I groaned.

'Well, after *you* took off yesterday, Lawrence was feeling proper bad about the whole ass-burger deal, what you yelled at him in the bog and all that, so he spoke to the headmaster—'

'The *headmaster?*'

'Yeah. Told him everything. He must have name-dropped too because Glen was pulled out of maths in the afternoon.

Word around the place is that he's been suspended till next week.'

'Hang on – they'd just suspend a kid like that without any witness cross-checking? Lawrence could have been lying, for all they knew.'

'Well, you did just disappear from school without telling anyone. I'm guessing they called your "in case of emergency" contact?'

Good old Caroline, I thought to myself, as I picked a crumb of morning crust out of my eye.

Tanya carried on. 'Problem is, Glen isn't as stupid as he looks. He quickly found out that Lawrence had snitched, and Glen being Glen, decided to get one back on him. Raffy, one of the lads who hangs out with Glen, lives in my block. He'd have well known that Lawrence is always poking around the back field by himself after school most evenings.'

It was getting more and more difficult to feel indifferent about the situation, but that didn't stop me from trying. This wasn't my fault, at all, just a really disgusting coincidence. Yes, that'll do nicely.

'Noel? Noel? Oi! Anyone home?'

I suddenly tuned in to Tanya's voice.

'Noel, seriously, I've just said your name, like, four times. Are your ears working or what?'

'Probably,' I said.

Another 11 bus glowed at us from the top of the road.

Tanya jumped to her feet. 'I've gotta get this one. Sure you're not coming?'

'No, go ahead,' I said. 'Have a good weekend. Tell Lawrence I said—'

'Whatever you wanna say, keep it for tomorrow morning. I'm gonna go check on him and you're coming too.'

As if *I'm* going to play Florence Nightingale to a hopeless case on a Saturday morning.

'No can do, Tanya. I'm extremely busy.'

'Ten o'clock outside the flats, Noel!' Tanya shouted over her shoulder as she ran down the road after the bus. 'You'd better be there!'

Back home, later that morning, I tried to make use of my bonus sick day by revising the elasticity of Rowntree's Fruit Gums, a task that had been on my To Chew list for a while. But my concentration kept failing. Worse than that, all these unwanted feelings kept showing up unannounced.

Confusion. Irritation. Anger. Frustration... Guilt.

Being alone in the house all day certainly didn't help things; there was silence everywhere.

I ended up falling asleep and was woken up in the late afternoon by the pinging of a message on my phone.

Tanya again.

No words.

Just a video link.

Something told me that this was going to be bad.

There were lots of reasons why I shouldn't have clicked on the link, but that's what ended up happening.

The blurry, hand-held images showed Lawrence being filmed from a distance in a field, while he was busying himself with his beehives. He had no idea he was being watched. Suddenly a group of lads whose faces were covered up with scarves ambushed him like a pack of wolves. Two of them pinned Lawrence to the ground. I watched him thrash about like a fish, screaming hysterically, while they kicked and smashed his beehives, using every bit of aggression and force they had. The camera made a final zoom in on Lawrence's tear-stained face, before cutting out.

You should know that I watched the entire harrowing video sequence without looking away.

But here's my confession: I muted the sound.

Because images alone can distress you, even terrify you, but sounds can haunt you forever.

15
The Importance of Being Lawrence

Of course, Tanya had to be late to our Saturday morning meet-up. And of course, the fact that she was late didn't bother her half as much as it bothered me, but I knew better than to make an issue about it. When she did make an appearance, at half ten, she led us round the back of her cinderblock to another cinderblock via a depressing-looking alleyway. We stopped in front of number twelve.

'Are you sure we're doing the right thing?' she asked as she knocked on the door.

Had she already conveniently forgotten that this was her idea to begin with?

'Let me do the talking. I've experience with showing up on doorsteps unannounced, as you know.'

Lawrence's mum answered the door far quicker than I'd anticipated. Going on first appearances alone, I can tell you that Mrs Lawrence is *very* different to Caroline. For example, Caroline has long, messy hair; Mrs Lawrence has short, well-brushed hair. Caroline isn't tall. Mrs Lawrence isn't short.

Caroline generally has a happy-go-lucky look about her. Mrs Lawrence looks as if she's just caught a whiff of fart.

No general pleasantries, such as 'Hello, are you here to see Lawrence?' or 'Hello, can I help you?' She just stood in the doorway and glared at us with eyes that seemed to telepathically warn us that if we didn't explain ourselves pronto, she'd call the police.

'There's no need to look at us like that, Mrs Lawrence,' I began. 'We're not the ones who ambushed your son, restrained him while his beehives were reduced to piles of wood splinters, before abandoning him next to the remains of his most treasured possessions. This is just a standard courtesy call, to see how he's physically and psychologically coping with the aftermath.'

We then politely pushed past Lawrence's mum, who was now looking heavenward, fondling the gold cross that hung around her neck.

It was easy to work out where the bedrooms were; the layout of the flat was exactly the same as Tanya's. One of the doors had a large homemade poster of a beehive with the words *INTRUDERS BEEWARE!* written on it.

Letting ourselves into Lawrence's bedroom, I was all set to be bombarded with bee paraphernalia (that's 'stuff' to those of you who can't cope with big words). I was braced for black-and-yellow colour schemes, shelves lined with hive smokers, queen catchers hanging from the ceiling, honey-scented beeswax candles, that kind of thing. But to my surprise, the room was almost empty. Just a bare desk with a cheap lamp and a stripped-down bed.

An icy wave of terror suddenly washed over me.

It must have doused Tanya too.

'Oh my God, Noel, he's dead! He's gone and topped himself! Well, I'm putting it on the record, this is *all* your fault. It's like a thousand per cent your fault!'

'*My* fault?' I panicked. 'You're saying that what happened to Lawrence is *my* fault? OK, sure, I shouted at him in the toilets and said some harsh-ish truths, but I never gave him instructions to go and tattletale to whoever would listen. That was *his* doing, Tanya. You can't argue with facts. Facts are facts!'

'He's right, Tanya,' uttered a voice from beyond the wall fixtures. We both leapt a foot in the air. I dashed over to a large wardrobe and flung it open. Lawrence was crouched down on a patch of flooring surrounded by stacks of cardboard boxes.

I didn't waste a second in communicating my overwhelming relief.

'Lawrence, what the hell is wrong with you?! Is that your pathetic attempt at some baseline humour? Well, it's a disgrace, as is the sight of you wallowing in a cardboard box pile of self-despair.'

Of course, Tanya's second X chromosome kicked in straight away and she held out a hand to help him up.

I was trying to prompt my brain to come up with something

suitably fitting to say to Lawrence, but all the lazy sod came up with was: 'I hope for your sake you don't feel as pathetic as you look.'

Tanya leant over to me and murmured, 'Getting it wrong, I *repeat*, getting it wrong.'

'What? Already?'

'Getting it *mega*-wrong, I promise you.'

It's true that Lawrence had started to whimper quietly to himself.

'Why don't you let me do the speaking from now on, OK?' Tanya said.

'Correction: *talking*. Fine, I'll let you do the *talking*,' I huffed.

Then the weirdest thing happened. Tanya reached out her arms towards Lawrence and hugged him. Out of nowhere, just like that. This made him cry even more. She clearly didn't have a clue what she was doing. Ugh, I wasn't handling this whole touchy-feely episode well at all. Too much physical contact. I had to put a stop to it.

'Here's a great joke: Jesus, Vishnu and the Prophet Muhammad walk into a—'

'Ssshhh!'

Tanya began throwing invisible darts at me with her eyes. Lawrence was really blubbing now – he'd soon have no water left in his body and shrivel up like a giant white raisin.

Then she said, 'I'm really sorry you've been through such a rotten time, Lawrence. That Glen's a right piece of work. Look,

I know that we've never talked much before, in school etc., but I want you to know that I'm here to help any way I can. Noel wants to help too, don't ya, Noel?'

'Noel?' sniffled Lawrence, looking up from Tanya's shoulder with a confused face.

'It's OK, Lawrence, you aren't suffering the after-effects of concussion or anything like that,' I assured him. 'Tanya's just dropped a d-bomb, that's all. By d-bomb, I mean dyslexia bomb. You see, Tanya here's dyslexic, so her brain can be quite partial to performing circus tricks with words, such as inverting the letters of my name. And while we're on the subject, it might interest *you* to know, Tanya, that Lawrence also has an autism spectrum disorder. This explains, among other things, his social clumsiness, his loner status, his overly keen interest in bees and his weirdness in general.'

'Way to big up the poor lad's spirits...' Tanya said as Lawrence continued to cry. 'Hang in there, mate. I'm sure your mum will speak to the school and they'll take care of things. Everything's gonna work out, you'll see.'

OK, that was enough.

'Mate? *Mate?* You're calling this one "mate" when you'd barely ever said a word to him less than forty-eight hours ago? And what's with all the comfort-the-crybaby canoodling? As if *that's* going to get him back to normal.'

'I can't do it!' Lawrence suddenly yelled, untangling himself from Tanya's arms. 'I can't do it! I won't do it! They can't make me. You can't make me!'

A matronly voice barked through the bedroom door keyhole, 'Lawrence, what's going on in there?'

'Nothing, Mrs Lawrence, Lawrence is in here with us, alive and well,' I reassured.

True, Lawrence was alive, but he was far from well. He was now shaking on the spot.

'I can't do normal; I'm fed up trying to be normal. Normal is *impossible*! IMPOSSIBLE!'

'Since when have you *ever* cared about being normal, Lawrence?' I said. 'You're the kid who likes bees more than Winnie-the-Pooh, how normal is that? Though come to think of it, Winnie-the-Pooh was more into the honey than the bees themselves…'

That started him off *again*…

'Of course I try to be normal!' he sobbed. 'I try to be normal *every single day*! I have no choice! How else do you survive school? How else do you make friends? How else do you avoid loneliness and meanness and hurt? If I had been "normal", I wouldn't have been so stupid when I spoke to Glen, so the whole ass-burger thing wouldn't have happened, so the whole Leon meltdown in the toilets wouldn't have happened, so I wouldn't have spoken to the headmaster to try and help out a friend whose reputation I'd destroyed without even realising it, and none of the rest would have happened either. The reality is I can't be my normal self and I can't be my fake normal self, so I give up. Done! Finished! Mum's agreed to have me homeschooled. She's calling the school on Monday.'

My heart sank down into my gut.

Lawrence was right. He was anything but normal. He was wholly kind and caring, and decent. Simply put, he was a good person. And, in case you haven't noticed, just like the bees, the world's population of genuinely good people is in steady decline.

I really wanted to tell Lawrence that he was important, even though he didn't think it. I wanted to tell him how bad I felt about what I'd said to him in my fit of rage and the suffering it had caused. Most of all, I wanted to promise him that I would find a way to fix things for us, but especially for him.

OK, here goes nothing.

'Lawrence, stop watering your Kleenexes and go find some proper clothes. We're off.'

I know what you're thinking... I'm working on it.

16
Candyland

'Well, at least it's not dinosaurs, I guess.'

It was a relief to hear Lawrence speak. He hadn't said a word since Tanya and I had managed to persuade his mum to let him outside. He was clearly too emotionally fragile to wander around in public, so I suggested we go to my place. Caroline was at work, so any awkward parental introductions could be conveniently avoided.

I, on the other hand, had just finished a twenty-minute introduction to my bedroom. I'd shown them my confectionery reference library, made up of over two hundred titles, and talked them through my extensive collection of maps that pinpointed local sweets that I'd tasted from specific geographical regions, including a map of all the rock candy varieties I've eaten around Blackpool – seventy-one and counting. They seemed most impressed (or weirded out, depending on how you interpret facial expressions) by my card cataloguing system, detailing every single type of confectionery that I've managed to track down across the globe. I'd say the current tally is near the ten thousand mark or so.

'What's wrong with dinosaurs?' asked Tanya. 'You scared of 'em? You know that they've been extinct for, like, billions of years?'

'Sixty-five million years,' I clarified. 'At the end of the Cretaceous period. By that time, they'd occupied the earth for approximately one hundred and sixty-five million years.'

'I know,' sighed Lawrence. 'That's what annoys me about dino-fanatics. They're always making a big deal about how dinosaurs were the first and only "cool" thing to happen to our planet. Bees have been around for more than a hundred and thirty million years *and* contributed massively to rebuilding the global ecosystem after the asteroid hit, but they don't have jaws that crush a car, so whatever.'

'Trainspotters are worse,' I said.

'There's *nothing* wrong with liking trains, Leon.' Lawrence scowled. 'Trains are super-interesting. I like trains. *Don't* insult trains.'

'Lawrence, anyone that gets a special fuzzy feeling thinking about a track change at Manchester Piccadilly is a freak.'

'Well, *you* get a special fuzzy feeling sucking on penny sweets – who's the freak now?!'

'That "fuzzy feeling" you're referring to, Lawrence, relates to the sensor receptors on my tongue, which decode the chemical compounds of whatever I'm eating. I'd only get a proper "fuzzy" feeling if the penny sweet in question had previously fallen on a rug, in which case, I'd never ingest it…'

'Conversation's getting a bit kooky, fellas,' Tanya cautioned as she stared off into space.

'Tanya's right, Lawrence. Let's talk about something else.'

'OK, but *promise* you'll lay off trains from now on.'

I took a moment to consider the request. 'Not possible. Especially when—'

'PROMISE!'

I looked across the room at Tanya. She'd pulled her head so far back in astonishment that she now had a treble chin.

A slow sigh wheezed out of me. 'OK, fine.'

Lawrence suddenly leapt forward and threw his arms around me. 'You're such a great friend!'

Panic.

'We're not friends, Lawrence.'

'You're right, Leon. We're not just friends. We're *best* friends.'

'Lawrence, we're not—'

'Hey! Guess what, Leon? I just realised something: you love sweets and I love bees... meaning you love sugar and I love honey...'

'Lawrence—'

Cue the high-pitched singing. *'Sugar... do do do do do do... oh honey, honey, do do do do do... you are my candy girl!'*

'I'm not a girl.'

'You are my candy boy!'

'I'm not gay.'

Lawrence stopped warbling. 'What?'

'I'm not gay. Well, come to think of it, I might be gay. I guess in order to know that, I'd first have to establish if I had any physical attraction to the opposite sex. To be quite honest, I've never given either avenue much thought.'

'And that's *my* cue to leave,' said Tanya.

'Why?' we both said simultaneously.

'Well, I wouldn't want to spoil the moment for youse… and also, if I'm honest, Noel, I'm a bit disappointed.'

'Why?' I asked.

Her eyes darted sneakily around my bedroom. 'Where's the stash?'

'What stash?'

'You're trying to tell me that you spend every minute of your spare time learning about sweets and things, but you haven't got a stash?'

'Oh, *that* stash. It's downstairs.'

'Downstairs? In a bungalow?'

'By its actual definition, Tanya, a bungalow—'

'*Noel*, my tummy's seriously growling, so you'd better lead us to a snack or something before I start growling for real.'

Fifty-two seconds later, we were standing in my underground storage facility – otherwise known as the bunker.

'This room's huge!'

Trust Lawrence to always be amazed by something.

'Apparently the man that used to live here before us was

particularly concerned with the threat of Armageddon. He then disappeared under mysterious circumstances. Caroline told me that when she first moved in, this room was filled with crates of tinned pineapple. It took her well over a year of eating them for breakfast, dinner and tea to get rid of them all.'

'Who's Caroline?'

'My mum, Lawrence. Nice lady, messy hair. Moving on—'

'This place is incredible, Noel!' said Tanya, visibly impressed. 'I've never seen so many... tiny drawers.'

'Two thousand, eight hundred and eighty-eight last time I counted.'

'How—?'

'It's pointless for either of you to ask questions before I've actually shown you anything, so listen carefully.'

'What's to explain?' asked Tanya, making a grab for a drawer marked *Rainbow Nerds*. 'Come on, I mean, we're literally in candyland here – let's get to it!'

I intercepted her hand. 'You can't touch those.'

'Ya what?'

'These sweets aren't for eating.'

'You're having me on!' she cribbed.

'Tanya, these are archives. All the sweets in these drawers are in vacuum-sealed packets.'

'What's the point of that?'

'Eh, to preserve them in case of an unexpected rise in humidity, or a rogue flood, blizzard or sandstorm... or from curious confectionery philistines with grubby hands. Seriously, Tanya, for someone who's prominently wearing the dyslexia badge of honour, you're really not doing your cause any favours with dunderhead questions like that.'

'Oi!' she snapped. 'You'd better shut that smart-arse mouth of yours, mate, before I rip off your goolies, roll 'em in icing sugar and eat them as bonbons!'

I dropped my eyes to the floor and cleared my throat. 'There's a fun pack of pickled onion Monster Munch in the kitchen cupboard. Follow me.'

As we made our way back upstairs, I'd just enough time to flex an out-of-sight smile. It may have been to express happiness at being called 'mate' for the first time in my life, or satisfaction at having managed to deter outsiders from tampering with my sacred stash.

Perhaps a little of both.

17
We're Not Forming a Club

'This is the most incredible thing… ever…'

'Lawrence. It's just a funhouse.'

'But it's in your back garden'

'Like I said. It's a funhouse.'

Lawrence was right; there was a funhouse in my back garden, a fact that I'd been trying to ignore with little success. The three of us were now standing in the long grass, staring up at the thing. Tanya had a look of bemusement, I had a look of indifference and Lawrence… well…

'It's a funhouse. It's a funhouse. It's a—'

'Let me guess. A funhouse?' said Tanya, tipping the last crumbs of her Monster Munch into her mouth. 'Seriously, boy, you gotta take things down a notch or you'll soon have apple juice trickling down the side of your leg.'

'I can't help it, Tanya. My echolalia kicks off sometimes when I'm overwhelmed..'

'Echo-watcha?'

'Echolalia – when a person repeats phrases or words said by another person, in quick succession,' I explained. 'It's a sort of verbal tic that affects some people who are autistic.'

Lawrence turned and beamed at me. 'You have tics too, Leon…'

'No, I don't.'

'Yes, you do…'

'No, I don't.'

'Yes, you do.'

'Oh yeah? Such as?'

'Such as, you're always moving your left hand – *constantly*.'

'No, I don't.'

'Yes, you do.'

'No, I don't.'

'Yes, you do.'

'Lawrence, my left hand is currently residing in the pouch of my hoodie.'

'But it's *moving*… I can hear it.'

'He's got a point there, Noel,' said Tanya. 'You're always fiddling around with something in that pouch. What you got in there? A gerbil?'

Cue moisture along the hairline of my forehead.

'First of all, I *don't* have a spasmic left hand. And no, I'm *not* housing a rodent ten centimetres north of my crotch.'

'Then what's in there?'

'*Relax*, would you? It's just some Jelly Babies, no big deal.'

Tanya made a face that assured me at almost 97.7 percent that her next spat of dialogue was going to start with the sentence *Are you for real?* She was predictable like that.

'Are you for real? Jelly Babies? So, what, do you like have some sort of off-the-charts Jelly Babies snacking obsession, or something?'

'No. I just carry them around.'

Lawrence huddled up disturbingly close to me with an enormous grin. 'Why?'

'Because.'

'Why?'

'Because.'

'Why?'

'Because.'

'Why?'

'Because.'

'Oi! Fellas? Are you planning to get off that merry-go-round any time soon? I swear, this place is beginning to feel more like a madhouse than a funhouse.'

And he was off again…

'A funhouse. It's a funhouse. Leon, you have a funhouse in your back garden. You have a *funhouse* in your back garden. We can hang out here together all the time. We can form a club!'

'Lawrence, we're not forming a club.'

'We can have a club name and a club crest and—'

'Lawrence, we're not forming a club.'

'And a club motto. Something really catchy, like "I'm Lovin' It".'

Tanya slumped down cross-legged into the grass. 'Hmm…
I'm liking the idea of the club… not so keen on the McSlogan.'

'Then how about—'

'Lawrence, we don't need a motto.'

'Yes, we do. It's part of being in a club—'

'Lawrence, we're not in a club. We're a bunch of kids whose
sole common denominator is that we are, through the eyes of
our peers, intolerably different.'

'JUST DO IT: that's a *great* motto!'

'Hence why it's already the slogan for the Nike clothing
company, Lawrence.'

'I know. Isn't it fantastic?? Maybe one day when we're
famous, they'll ask us to wear their clothes… for free…'

'Or they'll file a massive lawsuit. And to my knowledge,
they don't manufacture urban-style bee-keeping suits.'

'They might someday… when we're famous…'

'Lawrence, we're not going to be famous. Well, maybe
there's a chance that I'll become a household name when I
achieve international fame and notoriety for my expertise in
confectionery tasting, but that's a separate matter.'

'Names. We *have* to have secret club names for us as well.'

'We're *not* forming a club.'

'But we can't just have boring everyday names… we need
names that reveal our true identities. Who knows? Maybe one
day we we'll be made into… action figures!'

My elbows were seriously beginning to itch. 'Tanya, would

you please stop scribbling down there and come help me sedate Lawrence before he sprouts wings and flies off into the far-off cosmos?'

Lawrence suddenly let out a high-pitched squeal. 'That's it! *That's it*! From today, I'm no longer Lawrence Michael McCrory... I am... *Beeboy*...'

'And I'm done here,' I sighed.

'Me too,' said Tanya, putting the cap back on her marker and dragging herself to her feet. 'Check this out.'

Lawrence grabbed Tanya's sketch with both hands. '*The Asparagus Bunch – Just do it. Differently.* It's... brilliant!'

'No need to start hyperventilating again, Lawrence,' I said, as he began frolicking around the garden like a daft pixie. 'There's only so much a pair of human lungs can take.'

'What do *you* think, then?' Tanya asked, passing me over her sketchpad.

I took a look.

Goosebumps began wriggling up through the skin on my forearms.

'Differently is spelt with two fs,' I pointed out.

'Is that all you've got to say?'

'Fine. It's fine. I'm just not going to dwell on a concept that I have no interest in developing further.'

Tanya smiled sneakily back at me. 'Well, I can't take *all* the credit. Thanks for the inspiration, fellas, especially you, Beeboy.'

'His name is Lawrence.'

'Not any more by the looks of things,' she said. 'Oh, and you can call me Scribs from now on.'

'We're *not* forming a club.'

'Too bad, mate. Looks like we already have...'

18
Now What?

An omen, a premonition, a sign, call it what you want, but you should know that no sooner had Scribs (formerly known as Tanya) declared that we all now belonged to the Asparagus Bunch than the rain came. From out of nowhere. We listened to it plonk off the funhouse roof as we huddled together in the hall of mirrors on the first floor.

'Which of these mirrors makes me look the funniest?' asked Beeboy (formerly known as Lawrence).

'Now's not the time for those kinds of questions,' I said.

'Why?'

'Because as far as questions go, that one is completely pointless. Trivial at best.'

'All right, then, here's a question,' said Scribs. 'What do we do now?'

'What?'

'We've started a club – now what?'

'Oh, oh, I know, I know!' Beeboy yelled with feverish excitement. 'We can save the bees!'

'Come again?' quizzed Tanya (correction: Scribs.

Force of habit).

Beeboy's eyes zoned in on Scribs, like he was attempting to hypnotise her. 'Scribs, our friends the bees are in serious danger. Due to intensive farming practices, excessive use of agricultural chemicals and higher temperatures associated with climate change, the world's bee populations are rapidly declining. Did you know that in the past six years, more than ten million bee colonies across the world were lost to CCD, nearly twice the normal rate of loss? CCD is short for colony collapse disorder, which is when the majority of worker bees in a honeybee colony disappear, leaving behind their queen, and a few nurse bees to care for the remaining immature bees.'

Scribs seemed *genuinely* interested in what Beeboy was harping on about. Can you believe that?

'Hang on, where's the king bee? Has he left too?' Scribs asked.

Beeboy looked back at Scribs, stunned, then opened his mouth as wide as he possibly could to speak, but I gagged him with my sleeve.

'Get to the point, Beeboy, before you too find yourself without a colony.'

Beeboy nodded his head obediently before jumping to his feet and began pacing around the room, with dozens of his distorted reflections following him.

'We could put some beehives on the roof of the funhouse

and a little shed for me to keep my beekeeping equipment. Then I could make my own honey and sell it, with the proceeds going to the clubhouse's maintenance funds.'

'A hobby with the potential to produce an economic yield: approved,' I said.

'Fine with me,' said Scribs. 'I could set up an art studio in here. The natural light is quite good. And I could freshen up the walls around the place a bit. Paint a few murals, etc.'

'Oh yeah!' Beeboy agreed. 'What about a huge hall of fame mural that pays tribute to those great ND figures both past and present?'

I stared blankly at Beeboy. 'ND?'

'Yes. ND… as in neurodiverse. That's what we are. All three of us have brains that function differently, so we're part of the neurodiverse community.'

'Oh, for God's sake, Beeboy. Autistic. Asperger's. Autistic spectrum disorder aka ASD and now neurodiverse aka ND? What are you? A human label maker? Let's end this discussion. It's boring and unimportant.'

'Eh, says who?' Scribs wanted to know.

'Me. As founder of the newly formed Asparagus Bunch, it's my role to ensure that we keep our priorities (and therefore conversations) in order.'

'Club founder? Ya what?' Scribs laughed. 'Only ten minutes ago you were doing a big song and dance about *not* starting a club.'

'No, I wasn't.'

'Yes, you were! Like two hundred per cent you were.'

Beeboy did his best to clarify. 'Actually, Scribs, *I* was the one who was singing and dancing in Leon's room earlier on. But that was well over an hour ago.'

'Oh for… what I meant was that just ten minutes ago, Leon was totally against starting a club.'

'Well, as the saying goes, if you can't beat them, control them,' I said.

'Eh, don't think so… the saying's "If you can't beat them, join them".'

'Scribs, now's not the time to eenie meenie miney over words; we have serious business pending.'

'Like what?'

'Glen Jenkins.'

As soon as I'd said the words, Beeboy ducked for cover, covering his ears with his hands.

'It's OK, Beeboy, no need to be scared,' I tried to reassure him.

'No need to be scared?! Leon, Glen Jenkins is a harbinger of hell, no, worse than that, he's the overlord of the underworld, no, worse than that, he's the devil incarnate… no, no, *worse* than that, he's a *bully*!'

Beeboy was now circling around us like a shark.

'OK, OK, OK, Beeboy, step away from the flames. Look, you might think that Glen's all fire and brimstone, but to me he's just a pre-pubescent delinquent that needs to be sent packing.'

'You're gonna try and get Glen *expelled*?' said Scribs. 'Isn't that the school's job? How are you gonna manage that?'

'I think our club motto should provide us with a good point of departure… if we want to take down Glen Jenkins, we're going to have to do things differently.'

Scribs flashed a mischievous grin. 'You're really getting into this club thing, aren't you?'

'Well, there's no point doing anything in half measures now, is there?'

'If that's what you think, mate, then I think you should get yourself an official club name.'

'Yeah!' agreed Beeboy, much to my annoyance.

'There'll be *no* name baptisms taking place today,' I said in a frantic bid to curb their enthusiasm.

'Oh, *come on*, Noel,' moaned Scribs. 'Do us a favour and join in, would ya?'

'Negative,' I answered. 'As club leader, it is essential that I distinguish myself from you both, such as not adopting a stupid fake name. Look, it's vital we bring our ideas together and come up with a stellar plan to take down Glen Jenkins and restore order.'

Beeboy and Scribs both nodded in approval.

'Good. Now, here's the plan…'

19
Don't Be Scared, It's Only Revenge

'Maggie? Have you seen Caroline? Mag-gie? *Mag-gie*?'

For a split second, I thought the old hag was dead. Then, suddenly, she came to, jolting forward from her chair in surprise, taking in large gulps of air and coughing uncontrollably. It was like watching an exorcism. She eventually gestured with her stick towards the ghost train, so I scarpered, leaving her to do mortal combat with her respiratory system.

'Oh hello, lovie! What are you doing down here?' Caroline chirped when she caught sight of me cutting the queue.

'I need some advice.'

'Ooh. Can't it wait until steak and chips, tonight?'

'No, Caroline. I'm planning to get revenge on somebody in less than forty-eight hours, so my time is extremely limited.'

'Revenge? Really, Leon?' she sighed. 'All right, fine. But only one ride round, OK? You know that Saturday evenings are always chock-a-block.'

We hopped on the ghost train just before it departed. Once we'd passed through the wooden swinging doors and had been plunged into semi-darkness, I began.

'So, Caroline, to give you a brief overview—'

'Leon, I'm sorry, but before you launch into anything "brief", I'm putting my foot down.'

'But the ride's only started.'

Caroline buried her face in her hands. 'Aargh! Didn't Dr Snot send you a book about understanding idioms?'

'Not that I can recall.'

'Leon, you *cannot* get kicked out of Deluney.'

'Correction: moved on—'

'It's the same thing!' she shouted over the bloodcurdling screams. 'Leon, listen to me: there are *no* options left – apart from homeschooling, and I highly doubt that I'm the right person to be teaching you science and geography.'

'Agreed.'

'Or else we move to another part of the country. Which means I'll be out of a job and we'll have to start everything over. From nothing.'

Pre-recorded thunder and lightning crackled around us as machines pumped out strange-smelling synthetic fog.

'A lad named Glen Jenkins has been persistently traumatising a number of kids in my school.'

'You mean he's a bully?'

'He's not just your typical bully, Caroline. He's a sophisticated one. Quite astonishing given the way he puts a sentence together.'

'Has he been bullying you?'

'Caroline, now's not the time to ask hypothetical questions. Look, we've already passed the cycling skeletons. Anyway, I wanted to let you know that I've decided to do something about the situation. I'm going to seek vengeance on Glen, with the ultimate goal of getting *him* kicked out of Deluney.'

'Wait a minute. If this boy is being such a weasel, then why don't you just go and speak to the headmaster about it? I'll go with you, if you like.'

'Caroline, he's already been expelled from four other schools. Chances are he'll eventually get expelled from Deluney, only to be sent to another school and carry on his campaign of terror there. Vengeance is the only real solution.'

She eyeballed me in the dark. '*No* violence, Leon.'

'Caroline, when have I ever displayed violent tendencies?'

'True. Apologies. But to be honest, when I hear the words "vengeance" and "bully", violence is the first thing comes to mind.'

'Well, you can reassure yourself that my friends and I have—'

'Hang on, hang on, hang on… friends, Leon? Did you just say that you've got friends?'

'No.'

'Yes, you did.'

'No, I didn't.'

'Yes, you did!'

'Did you know that you have shockingly bad breath? As I was saying, *I* have come up with a plan that is genius in its creativity. It will catch Glen completely off guard.'

'BOO!'

'ARRRGGGHHHH!'

A gruesome-looking masked man with a blood-spattered kitchen knife jumped onto our wagon.

'Oh, my hairy Jesus!' screamed Caroline. 'Miguel! Now's *not* the time or the place! I'm having a serious conversation with my son here!'

'*Mil perdones*, Carolina...'

'To be fair, Caroline, I would have thought that riding through a ghost train attraction would be the perfect time and place to—'

'Oh, for crying out loud, Leon!'

'Correction, Caroline, *you* were one who cried out loud, not me...'

'I know, Leon! I know! Uh, that Miguel. He works over at the horror house, but he loves popping in here on his break for a laugh. I swear, we'll get a complaint one of these days.'

'I'll say. The ghost train is advertised from age three.'

The rickety wagons pushed through another door and we found ourselves back outside in the setting sunshine.

'Thanks for your time,' I said as we disembarked.

'Pleasure, as always,' she said, now a smidge calmer. 'Wait a sec. Didn't you say that you needed some advice?'

'Forget about it, Caroline.'

'No, seriously, Leon, what were you going to ask me?'

'Oh, nothing really. I only wanted to get your opinion on what type of revenge you think would be the most effective: sweet, sour, spicy or salty?'

'*Leon…*'

'Don't worry, Caroline,' I said as I put up my hood and disappeared into the crowds. 'No need to overheat your brain cells. I've already figured it out for myself.'

20
What's Up, Doc?

'Leon! What has you here so early in the morning? And how on earth did you manage to get inside the building?'

'You know what they say, Doc: the early patient catches the psychiatrist, especially when his hopeless receptionist isn't a morning person, and his cleaning lady takes pity on a boy standing outside his building in the rain without an umbrella.'

'Hmm,' said the doc, rummaging around in his trouser pocket for the keys to his office. 'Well, come in and throw your jacket onto a radiator for a few minutes, at least.'

'Correction, Doc: hoodie. I'll keep it on, thanks. The rain has already soaked through to my school shirt, but as I didn't have time to shower this morning, at least it'll have served a purpose.'

'And, eh, can I ask what the nature of your visit is today?'

I dropped a clear plastic bag of lozenge-shaped black sweets onto his desk.

'More liquorice, eh?' he said as he settled himself into his chair. 'That's very thoughtful, Leon, though I must admit, I've yet to make much headway with the first batch you gave me.'

I opened the bag and held it up close to his nose. 'Try one.'

'It's a bit early in the morning for me, thanks,' he smiled.

'Consider it a continental breakfast,' I insisted, rattling the bag.

The doc, a smart man, could sense that I'd no intention of backing down, so he begrudgingly took one and placed it on his tongue.

I waited for the standard five-second sensory delay.

Then right on cue, the doc's face started to shift and contort. He reached frantically for the wastepaper basket under his desk and spat out a mouthful of black gunge, before pulling a tissue from his box of Kleenexes and dragging it along his tongue, where it quickly began to disintegrate, leaving lots of little white specks on his bottom lip.

'From Helsinki with love,' I said. 'Delicious, aren't they?'

'What in God's name are those damn things?' said the doc, wincing in disgust.

'Those *damn* things? I'll have you know doc that *salmiakki* is the pride and joy of Finland, not to mention the wider Scandinavian community.'

'Salmi-what?'

I grabbed a fistful of sweets from the bag and tossed them in my mouth. 'Sal-mi-a-kki, a variety of liquorice flavoured with salt, otherwise known as ammonium chloride. These *salmiakki* pastilles contain 8.5 per cent ammonium chloride. The European Union currently regulates the use of ammonium chloride to 0.3 per cent in most foodstuffs, but there is no specific restriction for it in liquorice. Now, if your palate has been correctly trained to cope with the extreme levels of salt, *salmiakki* can be a gourmet delight, but to anyone else, eating these beauties can make you feel, well, like your body's nervous system is shutting down. That's why I've come to see you.'

'What for? To poison me?!' the doc grumbled, now scratching his tongue with his fingernails.

'To get your medical perspective,' I answered as I chewed. 'You're a genuine licensed practitioner, aren't you? Then you should be able to tell me how many of these sweets a person could eat in one go before hypernatremia sets in.'

'Hypernatremia?'

'Yes, hypernatremia. You know, a high concentration of salt in the blood. Severe symptoms include confusion, muscle twitching and bleeding in or around the brain.'

The doc gave me deadpan look. 'Now, why would you even want to know a thing like that, Leon?'

'I'm planning to get revenge on a kid in school later on today, so I just wanted to make sure that I don't run into any messy health insurance claims, legal harassments, etc.'

'You're planning to force-feed these things to someone in your school?!'

'Don't be so dramatic, Doc, would you? I'm hardly that way inclined. I'm just going to challenge him to a seemingly harmless sweet-eating contest, which he'll of course agree to without thinking, because he's an imbecile, and a big helping of salty revenge will be served up to him. The aim isn't to kill the cretin, Doc, just a bit of schadenfreude, that's all.'

'*Schadenfreude*?'

'Yes, schadenfreude – that wonderful German word that means to take pleasure in someone else's pain.'

The doc didn't seem to be relishing the idea quite as much as I was. 'Well, I do think that getting a chap to go through with a challenge like that, be it willingly or unwillingly, will surely put him through a great deal of pain.'

'So?'

'So, my point is, is that really the right thing to do?'

'Was it right for him to humiliate me on numerous occasions since I started at his school, Doc? Including one incident that saw my backside being using to flatten a hamburger that contained extra ketchup and mayo? Was it right for him to sadistically destroy my friend's beehives? The thing that mattered more to him than anything else in the entire world?'

Just like Caroline, the mere mention of the f-word made the doc smile from ear to ear.

'Leon, did you just say that you have a friend?'

'No. Yes. Maybe. It depends on the time of the day, the weather, the words that are coming out of his mouth, etc., but yeah, I guess you could call Lawrence a friend about 62.8 per cent of time, when he's not annoying the Snickers out of me.'

'And what about that girl you told me about?'

'Who? Tanya? Oh yeah, her. She's more of a mate than a friend.'

'What's the difference?'

'How should I know? What matters is that she's referred to me as her mate twice before, so I figure that it wasn't by mistake. She also let me touch her Afro the other day. That has to mean something, doesn't it?'

'Well, I must say that I'm really pleased for you, Leon. To have made friends that you feel compelled to protect and defend is quite something. Sounds like things are going well for you at your new school, and I'm delighted to hear it.'

'Whatever. I'll be more delighted when you answer my initial question. Do you want to try another one before making a final guesstimate?' I held out the bag again.

'No, no, I'm quite all right, thanks. You know, Leon, engaging in this type of… eh, how should I put it… liquorice warfare… is likely to have serious consequences for you.'

'Such as?'

'Well, I'm sure that your school wouldn't think twice about expelling you, especially given your track record.'

'Expel me?! Come on, Doc! This is liquorice we're talking about, not class A drugs.'

The doc pivoted slowly in his chair from side to side. 'While I fully understand your anger towards this chap, Leon, and your desire to make him experience the hurt and humiliation that he has put you and your friends through, I fear that you stand to lose a lot for just a few minutes of schadenfreude. In the long run, you'll be the ultimate loser in the story.'

'So, what are you suggesting? That I bow down before him and offer to rub his skanky villainous feet?'

'Not quite. What I suggest is that you don't act in haste. Take a bit of time to think of how you might be able to take care of this boy without putting yourself and your friendships at risk. You're a bright young man and your friend Tanya—'

'Mate—'

'Sorry, your mate Tanya seems to be a creative thinker too from what I've already seen. I'm sure that together you'll be able to figure it out.'

'Hmm... maybe... but in that case, I'll have to find someone to babysit Lawrence while we brainstorm ideas. Just mentioning Glen's name brings him out in an ugly rash.'

The doc smiled in approval and stood up to see me out. 'Nice seeing you, as always, Leon. I hope this meeting won't have you late for school.'

'It might,' I said. 'But Caroline will take care of that. It's her job, after all.'

'Ah, that reminds me. I bumped into your mother the other day in town. She introduced to me to Jim. Seems very nice.'

'*Gym?*'

'Yes.'

'Which gym?'

'What do you mean, which Jim? *Her* Jim.'

'You can't remember the name of the gym you saw Caroline in? Come on! There can't be that many of them around Blackpool. Have you seen how fat the locals are? Seriously, Doc, you'd want to get that short-term memory loss looked into. What I can't fathom is why Caroline would even be in a gym? I mean, it makes complete sense why *you* should be chained to a treadmill, but Caroline's never cared about her wobbly bits.'

The doc's cheeks turned a slight pinkish colour. 'Eh, so your mother has never mentioned anything to you about Jim. Never?'

'Does my reaction to what you've just said reflect anything to indicate the contrary, Doc?' I asked.

'Hmm… well, in that case, please feel free to pop by any time, Leon, if anything else comes up. I'm always happy to talk things through, if needed.'

'Thanks, Doc, appreciate it,' I said as I stuffed the bag of sweets into the pouch of my hoodie. 'Feel free to bill Caroline for the hour.'

Thankfully the rain had cleared off when I stepped back outside and headed in the direction of home. Yes, I know I was supposed to be on my way to school, but I figured that even if I jogged it, it would take me at least twenty-five minutes to reach Deluney, meaning I would be already ten minutes late for class. It seemed unfair to disturb everyone by arriving unannounced. Far better to just go home, sit out the first lesson and show up on time to the second. This would also allow me to watch the replay of last week's episode of *Mastermind*, my all-time favourite quiz show.

My feet pounded the pavement as I picked up the pace.

Caroline at the gym? This really was an intriguing one. There's no way she'd voluntarily subject herself to any form of physical exercise, even if she'd won a free lifetime membership in a sudoku competition. The information teased my brain all the way home and into the house, which still smelt of Caroline's morning serving of burnt toast. She was already out of the house – at the gym, I could only suppose.

I plonked myself onto the living room sofa and switched on the TV, expecting it to throw up an episode of *Come Dine With Me* or *Deal or No Deal*, or whatever lousy show was being shown on Channel 4, Caroline's favourite channel.

Hang on, what's this?

West Ham vs. Liverpool?

Sky Sports Premier League?

Just what was Caroline up to?

21
Evidence

'Noel, I'm *not* gonna say it again, put the knife and fork *away*!'

'What's it to you?'

'It's completely stupid!'

'Scribs, since when is eating food with a knife and fork stupid?'

'You're eating a Happy Meal!'

'Correction: pretending to eat a Happy Meal. I already had my meal before meeting you here.'

'Honestly, it's bad enough that you actually went and ordered us all Happy Meals in the first place. Why couldn't we have just gone splits on a Mega Meal? It would've been way cheaper!'

'Because then we'd have had to divide up the portions, which would have led to catastrophic breaches in hygiene protocol.'

'Why'd you not just order from the flippin' Value Menu, then?! We look like complete saps sat here with our little kiddie cardboard boxes.'

'If I hadn't ordered us Happy Meals, then we wouldn't

have gotten the toys.'

'Ya what? You telling me you did this *on purpose* because you wanted the ruddy toy?'

'Well, technically it's not a toy.'

Scribs pulled out a *Jurassic World*-themed Pez dispenser from her Happy Meal box and flung it into mine. 'Shoulda known.'

'You can have mine as well if you want, Leon,' said Beeboy as he mopped up the saucy remnants of his burger with a long, floppy chip.

'There's no need to offer, Beeboy,' I said. 'I was planning to take it. After all, it's thanks to my pocket money that you're savouring this feast, instead of that insipid mush they pass off for food at the canteen.'

OK, so it wasn't exactly the best place to call our first official club meeting to order, but you have to understand, this meeting was the most urgent of emergencies. It couldn't wait until a more convenient time at a more convenient place. I had made this very clear to Scribs and Beeboy by text earlier that morning and was glad to see them dutifully show up at the McDonald's just beside Blackpool train station. Yes, it wasn't the closest one to our school, but can I tell you for a fact that the McFlurries are way better churned.

'Getting down to business, I've called this club meeting because there is a sizeable issue that we need to get to the bottom of as soon as possible. Scribs, you following so far?'

'Eh-heh,' she replied, McSlurping her drink.

'Is this about Glen?' said Beeboy in a worried voice. 'It isn't about Glen, is it? He hasn't figured out where our clubhouse is, has he? He hasn't damaged it, has he? Is that why we're meeting here?'

'No, Beeboy,' I reassured him, 'it's *far worse* than that.'

'Far worse?!' they both said at the same time.

'What the hell could be worser than that?' Scribs said.

I leant down into my chips and signalled to them to join me.

'I'm under the impression,' I whispered, 'that Caroline might be considering the idea of seeking out a male companion.'

Scribs pulled back sharply from the huddle as if someone had just pinched her bum. 'What you on about?'

I sighed, in a bid to summon patience. 'OK, I'll give you the "for dummies" version then. *Boyfriend*. I think Caroline might be looking for a boyfriend.'

'*I got that, mate,*' she hissed at me with lashings of sass. 'What I meant was, why should we care?'

'Oh no! It's Glen, isn't it?' Beeboy shrieked. 'Caroline *can't* want Glen to be her boyfriend, Leon. He's the son of Satan! He's a – hey! What was that for?'

'You were spouting complete nonsense, Beeboy. A McNugget to the face was the only way to cut you off. Listen, this has *nothing* to do with Glen, except for the fact that the whole seeking-revenge-on-Glen plan will have to be temporarily shelved while we deal with this even bigger crisis.'

Scribs rolled her eyes. 'What? That your mum's after a fella? That's not a crisis.'

'Says the person who can't spell a word correctly if it contains more than six letters... of course it's a crisis, Scribs! Caroline has *never*, I repeat, *never* had a boyfriend. Never, ever, ever. I'm even pretty sure that my entrance into the world was via a stork whose GPS had failed. Caroline has never shown the remotest interest in having a companion. *I'm* her companion. And when I'm busy, she's got *Strictly*.'

'What makes you think she's on the hunt?'

'Exhibit A,' I said, pulling out a clear zip-lock bag from my rucksack.

Scribs gestured at me to hand it over. 'A can of lager?'

'An *empty* can of lager. I found it at the bottom of our bin this morning.'

'You went through your bin? You're insane!'

'No, Scribs, I'm thorough.'

'But that—'

'Don't even waste your breath. No, this can is not a staple drink in our home. Caroline drinks only two types of beverages: green tea and breakfast tea.'

'What about water?'

'Tea is water... murky water, and also, it was a lone can. So, answer me this, Scribs: why would a lady teetotaller randomly buy a single can of lager?'

'She—'

'*Exactly*. The only logical explanation is that *she* was accustoming herself with the taste of lager, so that she'd be able to order a pint in the local pub, where the vast majority of male Blackpudlians congregate.'

'That's ridiculous,' said Scribs. 'For all you know, someone tossed that can onto your front lawn and your mum had just put it in the bin.'

'Exhibit B,' I continued, producing another zip-lock bag.

'A TV remote?' said Scribs. 'So what?'

'Look closely,' I said.

'I don't see nothing. Beeboy?' She passed him the bag.

Beeboy took out the magnifying glass he always has in the front pocket of his rucksack in case he needs to study a bee up close.

'Hmm… it doesn't seem to be in any form of disrepair… Oh! There's a fingerprint on the back!'

'Full marks, Beeboy. You see, Scribs, that's why it's important to be thorough.'

'Yeah, yeah, whatever,' she grumbled, reaching for her McFlurry. 'So it's been used by someone with manky hands, who cares?'

'Well, for one thing, I care. But the more important question is how did the fingerprints get there?'

'I'm guessing the answer isn't because you or your mum were using the remote to watch TV, right?' Scribs said with no enthusiasm whatsoever.

'Exactly,' I answered. 'I'll have you know that this remote is the remote to our Sky box. We got a Sky box installed ages ago, but we've never used it. Not even once. This remote control has been in a sealed plastic sleeve in our coffee table miscellaneous drawer for nearly a decade. Now, it's suddenly out of the drawer, free of its packaging, and perched on the armrest of our sofa... complete with fingerprints!'

'So your mum's started using your Sky box!' Scribs moaned. 'Call me crazy, but that could be a possible explanation.'

'Which brings me to my third and final piece of evidence... When I turned on the TV this morning, the football came on. *Football*, Scribs. Trust me, Caroline would never put on the football by mistake; she has a strange phobia of zapping past channel nine on the TV. I think she's worried that if she zaps any further, she'll never be able to find her way back. And the football's on channel one hundred and eighty-two! You have to access it via a special menu!'

'Look, mate, what are you getting at with all of this? You might have had the morning off, but we've been in school. You're wasting our entire break on this waffle!'

'Scribs, how are you not able to keep up with the simplest of conversations? Evidence! This is further evidence that Caroline is on the lookout for a boyfriend. She's trying to familiarise herself with football so she'll be able to strike up a conversation with a lager-chugging, footie-mad alpha male. It's a well-known fact that a minimal knowledge of the beautiful game considerably increases a woman's chances of appealing to men from the north. That and darts.'

Scribs's mood cooled as she considered the evidence more seriously. 'I still don't get it, Noel. I mean, why all this sniffing around all of a sudden?'

'I was speaking with my doctor this morning and he let it slip that he'd seen Caroline in town the other day and that she'd introduced him to gym. Oh, that's another *huge* piece of evidence I forgot to mention earlier.'

'Jim? Jim who?'

'Not *Jim who*, Scribs. What you actually wanted to say was *which gym*?'

'No, I didn't—'

'I'm pretty sure I understand the mechanics of the English language *a lot* better than you, Scribs. No offence, of course.'

'*Of course…*'

'And to answer your intended question, no, I don't know which gym Caroline's faffing around in. It was enough of a shock to hear that Caroline actually knows that gyms exist, let alone that she's signed up to one.'

Beeboy was still inspecting the remote control up close.

'Leon, does Caroline have particularly large thumbs?' he asked.

'No,' I answered. 'Quite the opposite actually. Hence why she can never manage to peel an orange correctly. It's very unpleasant to watch. I've taken to leaving the room when she takes one out of the fruit bowl.'

Beeboy and Scribs swapped a concerned look.

Strange.

Maybe they're both esperidoeidiphobic and have a chronic phobia of citrus fruits. Now that *would* be a coincidence.

'Mate. D'you know what? Why don't you drop the detective work for a bit, yeah? Might be good if you focused on something else?'

'Good idea,' I said. 'It's pointless carrying on investigating, I've already unearthed a staggering amount of evidence. Now we must leap into action.'

Scribs cringed. 'Action?'

'Yes. We need to go down to the promenade this afternoon after school so that I can confront Caroline in person.'

Beeboy began whimpering. 'But… why do we have to go? I don't like confrontations. I don't like the noise, Leon. I *really* don't!'

'Beeboy, I need you and Scribs there with me to act as official witnesses. OK, so you didn't help me uncover the evidence, but Caroline doesn't need to know that. There won't be a dramatic confrontation. Technically, Caroline hasn't betrayed her only child yet, but these pieces of evidence have made it clear that she's thinking about it. Tackling the issue head on by ambushing her when she least expects it is the best way of extinguishing these silly notions before they gather strength.'

Scribs was now twiddling her thumbs awkwardly in her lap. 'Eh, mate, d'you not think your mum might already have a—'

'Scribs! Please! I've got a foolproof plan that's nicely cementing itself in my head. Don't go mucking it up with your messy thought prints.'

'Whatever,' she said, taking her blazer from the back of her chair. 'Best be off if I'm to be back in time for the bell. Beeboy, you coming?'

Beeboy scurried to grab his things. 'You're coming too, aren't you, Leon? Everyone at school will be wondering where you are.'

'Negative, Beeboy,' I said. 'I'm going back home to rehearse what I'm going to say to Caroline when I see her later on. But I'll be waiting for both of you at the usual bus stop after school.'

We parted ways. Scribs and Beeboy headed back to Deluney to be taught nonsense by some mediocre teachers, while I was preparing to teach my own mum a thing or two – namely that her darling son, Leon John Crothers, is a bona fide genius.

Nothing, absolutely nothing, gets past me.

22
The Sweet Stench of Death

'Almonds. I smell almonds.'

'What you on about, Beeboy?' said Scribs.

I sniffed the air. 'Beeboy's right. There's a smell of almonds. Buttery almonds.'

'Ooh! Ooh! And a hint of… oh, what's it called?'

'Primark.'

'What?'

'The word you're looking for is Primark, Beeboy.'

'No, I wasn't. I was thinking of patchouli, which is—'

'An aromatic oil obtained from a South-East Asian shrub from the mint family, commonly used in perfumery, insecticides and medicine. It also happens to be one of the overpowering scent notes to Primark's Polka fragrance, a poor man's version of Paco Rabanne's Lady Million, alongside hints of neroli, jasmine and gardenia, mixed with amber and bitter orange.'

'Seriously, *what* are youse on about?' said Scribs, now sniffing the air as well. 'All I can smell is scummy water.'

I'd had no luck reaching Caroline on her phone as our bus

crossed the city centre and dropped us off at Bond Street. From there, Scribs, Beeboy and I walked down Withnell Road and onto the promenade, which was busier than usual for a Monday evening. Loads of 'summer's not over' militants in shorts and flip-flops.

The three of us were now sitting in a makeshift log boat, meandering along a gentle rapid inside the River Caves water ride in the heart of Blackpool Pleasure Beach. Maggie had indicated to us that Caroline was manning the River Caves attraction this evening, and as the old heifer is almost always right, when there was no sign of her at the front of the line, I suggested we go looking inside the attraction itself. Chances were some drunk idiot had fallen overboard trying to propose to his cousin in the Tunnel of Love and she was in the middle of trying to fish him out of the water with a big net.

'Ah… enhanced olfactory sensitivity… another great superpower we share!' Beeboy chirped as he continued to flex his nostrils.

'What? You mean that you both smell things really well?' said Scribs.

'Both the pleasant and the vile,' I confirmed. 'Though it's far from being a superpower. Who really wants to catch a whiff of a bad wipe job wafting out of a lad's boxers as he outruns you for the bus?'

'Oh my God! You are rotten!'

'Though, I guess a heightened sense of smell does have its

advantages in certain situations. Such as right now.'

'What d'you mean?'

'Well, if you take the scent of almond hand cream and combine it with a few too many spritzes of Primark Polka, you've got Eau de Caroline, which means she's close by.'

No sooner had I said those words than my ears picked up a shrill giggle, followed by an unladylike snort. It echoed around the Inca caves that we'd just floated into.

Without thinking, I jumped from the wooden boat onto the nearest plastic rock formation. Scribs and Beeboy followed. We slowly edged our way along the scenery's narrow, slippery ledge towards a nearby waterfall before ducking behind it.

The first thing I saw was Caroline's slouchy denim bag on the ground, and her completely non-essential handbag essentials scattered all over the place.

Then I saw Caroline.

She was leaning up against the grotto wall, her arms wrapped around some big man-creature. And they were... ugh, let's just leave it there, shall we? I'm all for censorship in these sorts of situations. After all, if I do go into any more detail, then Amazon will go loco and say that I'm not respecting the appropriate content for the book's marketed age range, meaning that I'll be banking less cash.

At first, I was so taken aback that I didn't know what to do. Neither Caroline nor the big man-creature had even twigged that I was standing within gawking range. I eventually figured

I should make my presence known, so I coughed loudly and Caroline's head whipped round.

'Leon!'

'Caroline.'

'What… how?'

'I figured that now might be a good time to make some introductions.'

'Eh, you sure about that?' whispered Scribs, who was now at my side with Beeboy. 'Because I'm not.'

Both of them were using their hands to block out the smoochy vision from their eyes.

'Don't worry, it won't take long. Caroline, I'm pleased to introduce you to Tanya and Lawrence, two very decent human beings I go to school with. Tanya, Lawrence, I'm *far less* pleased to introduce you my mum, Caroline: Sagittarius. Leftie. Tart.'

'Leon!' Caroline gasped.

'Easy, lad,' said the big (apparently cockney) man-creature, as he wiped some sticky gloss from his thick moustache.

I pivoted my head slowly in his direction.

'Couldn't agree with you more, *geeza*. Caroline *is* easy. She's also disorganised, simple-minded and has *appalling* personal hygiene, with a special mention going out to the fungal infection she's been cultivating on her feet for the past seven years, meaning that her toenails look like cornflakes. I swear, watching her attack those things with clippers is a sight to behold.'

'Gross!' blabbed Scribs.

Caroline's face dropped. 'Leon. How could you... how could you say something like that?'

If she thought she was going to slow down my momentum, she had another thing coming.

'It isn't difficult, Caroline. All I had to do was think about what I wanted to say, open my mouth and then say it. I understand that for you the concept might be a bit far-fetched. You who rarely thinks before doing anything... case in point... knocking around with this dumb-looking sod.'

'Stop it!' she yelled. '*You!* You listen to me! I am *not* knocking around. This is Jim – my *boyfriend*. He's been my boyfriend for the past *eight months*. Jim is a decent, lovely man, who has *always* treated me with respect. You should treat him with respect. You should treat me with respect too because *I am your mother!*'

I allowed my brain an extra moment to properly transcribe the earth-shattering information I'd just received onto some memory parchment.

'OK, Caroline. Note taken. But a minor edit to your last remark... *were*... you *were* my mother once upon a time, but as of right now, you are no longer. In fact, you no longer exist. And I think I speak for the entire human race when I say the world will be *far* better off as a result.'

Her hand swiped full force across my face.

The gushing noise from the nearby waterfall was now the

only sound.

I looked directly into her wetting eyes as I felt the sting pulsate along the surface of my skin.

My saving grace came in the form of a well-positioned emergency exit embedded into the grotto wall, just behind Caroline. I walked straight past her and pushed through the metal door.

Outside, in the real world, I was met with the same recognisable sights, sounds and smells, but I felt like a completely different person.

That was it.

Caroline was dead, meaning I was now an orphan.

Things I will miss about Caroline:
1. Her messy hair
2. Her deep-fat frying
3. Her whistling
4. Her knitting
5. Her indiscreet nose-picking
6. Her sardine-wrapped olives
7. Her

23
The Unknown

Grief is a complicated thing. Well, at least that's what Google says.

Apparently, there are five stages to coping with loss: denial, anger, bargaining, depression and acceptance... in that order. These stages are supposed to linger for varying lengths of time. Some articles I read online were speaking about years in certain cases... what a complete waste of a lifespan that is! There was no way I was going to give Caroline the satisfaction by sacrificing all that time pining after what we used to have together. The good news was that in the space of less than an hour, I'd already managed to cross off the first stage of grief from the list: denial. Scribs and Beeboy had asked me on the bus ride home if I was OK after what had happened and I said I was fine when, of course, I wasn't.

Now, back at home, in the privacy of my own room, I could move on to the next stage: anger. As you know, there are lots of different ways that a person can evacuate their pent-up rage. Some people punch pillows, some punch their nearest and dearest, some nutcases even punch themselves. Personally, I don't go in for that sort of thing. When I'm angry, when I'm very, very angry, I eat Curly Wurlies. Trust me, there's nothing better than wrangling that latticed chocolate-coated chewy caramel bar between your teeth, using your incisors to pull off long sticky strands and then grinding them down with your back molars until your jaw muscles are spasmed and throbbing.

But even with five Curly Wurlies in my system, I still had an empty feeling in the pit of my gut. Turns out my well-conditioned appetite was expecting its Monday evening helping of fish and chips promptly at 8 p.m. Caroline had left my tea on the counter to be re-heated before she'd left for work that afternoon, but there was no way I was going anywhere near that. Who'd want to eat food that had been prepared by someone who was, for all intents and purposes, dead?

There wasn't even the possibility of popping out to the chippie. A previous incident there, involving myself and a so-called derogatory comment to the chippie's Irish owner, has me banned for life. In the end, I found a tub of fish-food flakes under the sink from a once-upon-a-time pet we had and sprinkled them into a large bag of salted crisps.

As I ate, my brain motored on, trying to process this latest shocker. So many uncertainties. I jotted a few of them down on a piece of kitchen roll to take the pressure off my emotional bandwidth.

Things that remain unknown:

1. How did Caroline manage to lead a mysterious double life for so long?
2. For just how long was Caroline planning to lead a mysterious double life?
3. Has 'he' ever used our bathroom? And if so, for what purpose?
4. When will the Americans ever stop trying to kid themselves that their sacred Halloween snack, candy corn, is the best candy in the world? The things taste like melted wax crayons.
5. How can I get revenge on Glen Jenkins without getting kicked out of Deluney?

My stomach suddenly heaved. I needed to get some air, so I stuffed the kitchen paper into the back pocket of my jeans, grabbed an extra hoodie to protect myself from the late evening chill and wrestled Caroline's bike out from the pile of outdoorsy junk that cluttered up the porch.

As I cycled along the pitch-black roads, my insides churned in sync with the rotating wheels; apparently my directionless pedalling was only making things worse. So, I chose a suitable destination and picked up the pace.

Four kilometres and three flights of stairs later, I was banging on Scribs's front door.

A strange noise from inside the flat that sounded like a fox in heat got louder and louder until the door opened violently.

Standing on the threshold was a version of Scribs, except with less enormous hair and more enormous boobs.

'You're not Tanya,' I said.

'Ya what?' she barked back. 'Who the hell are you and what are you playing at ringing round here at this hour?'

'Why are you people always so loud?'

'*Ya what?!*'

'Seriously, you all have an ignorance to your vocal cords that boggles the mind.'

'*What you say?* Dev! Dev! Get out here!'

Uh-oh.

Thankfully Scribs appeared at the door before the summoned 'Dev' – whom I'm assuming was Scribs's never-before-mentioned hard-ass 'bruva'.

'Noel, what are you doing here?'

'Tans, you know this one?!'

'Yeah, yeah, it's fine, Denise, just leave him, all right? He's decent.'

'Decent?! You mad? He's a grief-giving racist little—'

'Whatever he said, he didn't mean it. He just says things sometimes that he shouldn't. We're working on it.'

Scribs then ushered the wailing banshee back to her bedroom before stepping out into the corridor, leaving the door on the latch.

She looked at me, bleary-eyed. 'Go.'

I turned and headed towards the stairs.

'I *meant* "go" as in "go on, I'm listening".'

I stopped a few steps down and looked back up at Scribs in her ugly, tropical-fruit-themed pyjamas. 'No, it's OK. See you around.'

'Oi! You did *not* get me out of bed this late on a school night and start a beef with my older sister Denise just to say "See you around." So you'd better say whatever it is you came here to say, or you won't see the morning!'

'I don't really have anything to say,' I told her. 'I wasn't feeling good at home, so I thought I'd go for a cycle, and, well, you know, grim thoughts tend to lead to grim places, etc.'

'Charming.' She yawned as she beckoned me back over. 'Look, I understand that you're upset with your mum—'

'I'm not upset, Scribs. I'm raging, fuming, incensed, infuriated, *seething*—'

'OK, so you're *really* upset. Life has just given you an unexpected slap across the face, that's all.'

'Scribs, do you think this is all about money? Maybe Caroline was strapped for cash and thought that getting a man was a way to ease her financial troubles? If that was the case, then I could have just quit school and gone back to working confectionery quality control at the Pleasure Beach. The faded gumballs in the machine beside the Derby Racer alone are a red flag to *any* health and safety inspector.'

'Hmm… not quite sure what you're on about, mate,

but you'll be all right, trust me. It'll just take a bit of getting used to.'

'Used to what?'

'To your mum's new fella. Who knows, he might even turn out to be a decent bloke, like my mum's boyfriend, Dev. He's been living with us for about four years now and I actually like him. He puts up with us lot, makes Mum happy and all that jazz.'

'Well, good for you Scribs, that your mum's boyfriend is a talented musician, but there's no way I'm getting used to this. I'm pretty sure the only music that this "fella" knows how to make is through his back passage.'

'Lost me again—'

'Doesn't matter. It's not going to change anything. My life's gone down the plughole and I'm just going to have grin and bear it.'

'Well, I'm sure if you talk to your mum and say you're sorry, she'll understand. It was a kinda crazy situation, to be fair.'

'Scribs, Caroline is dead. And I'm not interested in communicating with the afterlife; best let the dead get on with their eternal happiness, or eternal suffering, or in Caroline's case, limbo-ing festively between the two.'

'You know, mate, sometimes I wonder if you can't get any weirder and then you come out with corkers like that.'

'*How* could I have not seen this coming? You know, all of this has made me realise that I knew surprisingly little about Caroline.'

'Well, you knew about her toenails – that's pretty cosy... not to mention dis-gus-ting.'

'That's nothing,' I said. 'She's also got clusters of raised purple veins on the sides of her thighs that look like neurotic Spirograph doodles.'

'Oh, God, Noel! Give it a rest, would ya? I have to sleep tonight.'

'Fine. I'll go home, where I can guarantee you that I will *not* sleep tonight. But this talk has been beneficial. If anything, it has enabled me to pass through the bargaining stage of grief, leaving me with just depression to go before it's acceptance and then happy days.'

'Too tired to ask, mate. I'll just cross my fingers that you've got whatever's jamming around in your noggin under control.'

She then said goodbye and sleepily waved me off down the stairs.

All the lights were out in the bungalow as I freewheeled into the driveway, a bit after 11 p.m. I clocked Caroline's dusty white van, lobbed up on the kerb outside. Thankfully she'd seen sense and buggered off to bed, allowing me to brush, floss and flush undisturbed before settling under my warm duvet to impatiently await the arrival of the great depression.

'Leon?'

Oh fudge.

Caroline.

Her slippers hissed along the hallway towards my bedroom door, which was slightly ajar.

'Leon, can I come in?'

I dove out from underneath the covers and hurtled myself towards the door, forcing the latch firmly into its lock box.

I thought that such an aggressive move would see her off back to her room, but instead I listened to her woolly-clad backside slide down along the length of the door right down to the floor.

Now what? Was she just going to sit there outside my room and wait for me to change my mind? Would I have to barricade myself inside for days on end and eventually initiate a hunger strike for her to step aside?

'Things that remain unknown.'

OH FUDGE.

'Question one: How did Caroline manage to lead a mysterious double life for so long?'

But I could have *sworn* that I'd stuffed that list into my pocket before heading out. Just my luck.

'Um, to be fair, Leon, I didn't go out of my way to lead a mysterious double life,' Caroline said in a meek voice. 'It was something that just grew over time. I've known Jim for ages. He's been working at the Pleasure Beach almost as long as I have and we've always enjoyed a joke when we bump into each other around the grounds, nothing more. Then round about Christmas time, there was a shift in the universe or something like that and we started to see each other as something more than we did before.'

Hang on a second… *Jim*? As in 'one in a gazillion' Jim? The Jim who dumped that freak hut in my back garden?!

'Question two: For just how long was Caroline planning to lead a mysterious double life?' she continued. 'Well, it's true I'd been putting off telling you about Jim for a while. I guess I felt that with a new, new, new, new, new, new, new school change at the end of the summer and then with the autism stuff on top of that, you were already dealing with a lot. I should have been upfront and honest with you from the beginning so that this didn't all come as such a shock, especially that things between me and Jim are getting, well, serious, I guess you could say.'

And just what does she mean by that?! Oh, I can see it now. Moving boxes, his-and-hers bathroom sinks, a topless beer belly at the breakfast table with huge helpings of 'Don't mind me, mate!'

'Question three—'

Please skip that question…

'Has "he" (I guess that means, Jim) ever used our bathroom? And if so, for what purpose? Jim has been around at the house a few times when you were at school and he did use the bathroom a couple of times. I never asked him for what purpose, but I can tell you that he has never left any smelly clues in there behind him. Hopefully that will make you feel a bit better.'

Yes, thank you, Caroline, I feel Snickerloads better now.

'Um, I'm not so sure about question four. But I know that the Americans have a saying, "If it ain't broke, don't fix it", so I'm guessing that candy corn is sticking around?'

Not if my future adult self has anything to do with it. Stupid Yanks.

'Question five…'

…

I waited.

…

Nothing.

…

Still nothing.

…

Sniffling.

…

Quiet crying.

'Question five.'

Less quiet crying.

'Oh, for gosh sakes, trust me to start blubbing at the worst possible time!' she blubbed. 'I'm sorry, Leon, for… for…'

Caroline's emotions were now starting to take the upper hand, so I was enormously relieved when she decided to put us both out of her misery.

'Let's sit down together tomorrow and talk everything through,' she whispered through the door. 'OK, lovie?'

I didn't bother answering. I just sat in silence at the foot of my bed and played the waiting game until she caved after seven minutes and left without saying another word.

As soon as I climbed back into bed, stage four hit me like a ton of bricks, almost crushing me into the mattress.

He actually used the bathroom. *My* bathroom. OK, technically it's Caroline's bathroom as well, but its governance is overseen by *me*. No, the carpet will *not* be pulled up and replaced by cold, heartless, slip-inducing tiles. No, we will *not* burn cheap incense to cover up lingering odours – they should be allowed to evaporate naturally by themselves. No, we *cannot* include *Closer* magazine in the stack of reading material beside the toilet. A copy of the Argos catalogue is my absolute limit.

Then, just like that, my brain switched off completely, catapulting me into a profound sleep, but not before signing off with one last thought:

Life is like a marshmallow. Easy to chew but hard to swallow.

24
Depression

'Cheer up, mate. You're seriously not gonna stand at your locker with a face like that all day?'

'Quite possibly.'

'How's about Beeboy and me get you something from the machine? What you fancy?'

'Does the machine now stock packets of Special K? Not the chocolate bits one or the red berries one – the original.'

''Fraid not.'

'Forget it, then.'

Believe me when I say that school was absolutely, categorically, the last place I wanted to be right now. Last night's events were still weighing down heavily on me. If I'd had my way, I'd have been back home, buried under the bedcovers but that would have meant being confronted again by the red-headed she-demon. I even had to skip breakfast for the first time in my life and shimmy out of my bedroom window to escape from the house unseen.

'Well, I'm all out of ideas,' Scribs sighed. 'You don't even seem bothered with the Oasis *Morning Glory* CD I dug out of our storage locker for you. FYI, you know you're like the last person on the planet who doesn't listen to music on their phone. Anyways, I thought you'd be chuffed, seeing as how much you bang on about Noelie G.'

'Noel's got good life insights, but to be honest, Scribs, I couldn't care less about his music or his band.'

'What?'

'I've already told you, I'm not much of a music person... at all... ever.'

'How can you say that about Oasis?! Oasis songs aren't just "songs", they're like proper anthems!'

'Anthems?'

'Well, yeah! Anthems to all of life's craziness. I'm telling you, mate, listen to that CD, and it'll all become clear.'

'OK, I'll put it on my maybe list. Though I stress that it's a *maybe* list, Scribs, which means I'll probably never listen to said CD, so don't go pestering me under any circumstances. You've been warned.'

'All right, this skipping breakfast malarkey is doing you no favours. You need sugar, mate. What d'you want? Mars? Aero? What about a Bounty?'

'*Bounty?!* I'm going to pretend I didn't hear that.'

'I love Bounties!' said Beeboy. 'They're so yummy and full of coconutty goodness.'

OK, there was *no* way I was having that.

'Beeboy, carry on bigging up Bounties like that in my

presence and you'll be getting a swift kick in the coconutties.'

'Oi!' shouted Scribs. 'You gonna drop the attitude? I swear, even the Bounty bar is getting a bashing this morning.'

'Wise up, would you, Scribs? A Bounty is *not* a bar. It's actually *two* chocolate bars – *plural* – sneakily packaged to resemble a chocolate bar, for some insane reason that only the head honchos at Nestlé know. Why do a thing like that? Why two separate bars? Why doesn't the Bounty just toe the traditional chocolate bar line, like Snickers, or Mars or Galaxy? Or else own up to its cocoa-coated lover and be packaged accordingly, like Twixes or Twirls or Kinder Buenos? Its suspicious, Scribs, that's what it is. Bounties are suspicious. And as you might have guessed, I'm not in the mood for suspicious behaviour, be it from my recently deceased mother or *any* mass-produced confectionery product.'

It seemed like that was one negative comment too many for Scribs.

'Right, Noel, I'm gonna give you a harsh truth talk here, so buckle up.'

That didn't sound good. And to make matters worse, Scribs had now crossed the imaginary circle of distance I try to keep between myself and others. So, this is what she must mean when she says, 'And then I got all up in her face...'

'*Reality check, Noel:* everyone goes through bad stuff in life. Scary stuff. Sad stuff. Unfair stuff—'

'Repetitive stuff,' I said, using my hand to mime a signal for her to hurry the hell up, so that she'd step back out of my discomfort zone.

'The best way to get through this bad stuff, and come out the other side feeling better and stronger, is to accept that in life *BAD STUFF HAPPENS*! And another thing: *stop* saying your mum's dead, would ya? Seriously, you'll be zapped by a thunderbolt if you carry on like that.'

'Well, it's a good thing that God made me an atheist, now, isn't it? But going back to what you just said... the whole having to accept life's hard knocks, etc., I couldn't agree with you more.'

'Really?'

'Absolutely. Acceptance is what it's all about. Am I right?'

'Well, yeah.'

'So, in that case you'll agree that Caroline is just going to have to accept that after thirteen years of co-dependence with me, her only child, she can't just suddenly change the rules because it suits her.'

Scribs looked worried.

'That wasn't what I was getting at, Noel—'

'Of course you weren't. But that's what I'm getting at.'

'You're not gonna tell your mum that she can't have a boyfriend... because you said so... are you?'

'More or less, yes.'

'Not sure how well that's gonna go down...'

'Don't get your Afro in a frizz; I've no plans to hire a hitman or send Caroline a severed finger in the post. My strategy is going to be far more subtle.'

'Meaning?'

'That I'm going to move out.'

'Move out? Of your house? You serious?'

'Yes. It will send a clear message to Caroline that I'm fully rejecting her recently updated relationship status.'

'Where you gonna live, then?'

'You can come live with me, Leon,' said Beeboy. 'We have lots of space in my flat, I'm sure my mum won't mind, she'll get to like you some day, I'm sure she will, and that way we can be friends *and* roommates. We could be froommates!'

'Beeboy, what you've just said confirms at eight thousand five hundred per cent why you and I could never cohabit in the same space, even if said space happened to have the land mass of Jupiter,' I snapped. 'Look, I don't want to talk about this anymore. I'm hungry and my energy levels are low. In fact, let it be known that as of now I'm going to cease all communication until after dinnertime, to avoid uselessly burning up any more calories.'

'You know,' said Scribs, 'I read somewhere that coconuts give you a *huge* energy— OUCH!'

A sharp pinch on the upper arm – that'll teach her.

25
Good Riddance, Caroline

I soldiered on through the rest of the school day with incredible discomfort. I may have come up with a plan, but that didn't soothe the horrific throbbing sensation that was coming from my chest. What was that all about? I hoped I didn't have a cancerous tumour the size of a tennis ball playing peek-a-boo behind my ribcage; that's all I needed right now. Mind you, if that were the case, then maybe Caroline would cop herself on and things would just get back to normal.

Scribs and Beeboy did their best to boost my morale. Beeboy even did an impression of the mating dance of the East African lowland honeybee (or the *Apis mellifera scutellate*). Scribs laughed herself stupid, but I wasn't feeling it. I was feeling agitated. Agitated and paranoid. My mind was still ransacking my memory bank, trying to draw up flashes from the recent past where something may have seemed out of place.

Last week, for instance, I distinctly remember thinking to myself that a carton of milk in our fridge had been opened differently. Caroline usually snips off the corner of the carton with scissors, leaving just a little hole at the spout (on my request) so that it doesn't draw in strong food odours from the fridge. This carton, however, had a massive clumsy tear instead, which made for sloppy pouring. Did *he* do that? Or what about that time a few weeks ago when I could have sworn that the DVDs on the storage unit under the telly had been tampered with? I definitely remember flinching when I spotted not one but *two Mrs Brown's Boys* compilations facing upside down. Our DVD player's been on the blink for years now, but that doesn't stop me appreciating that our DVDs are lined up properly on the shelf and standing the right side up. Was *he* browsing our DVD selection? Is *he*, like Caroline, an unashamed fan of live comedy series featuring a grown man cross-dressing as a working-class OAP? He'd better not.

I had to find somewhere new to live, as soon as possible. On my way home on the bus, I whittled down the possibilities.

Alternative places I could live:

1. ~~A family member's house~~ (Caroline is family. The buck stops there)
2. ~~Scribs's house~~ (Angry sister and potentially intimidating parental figure named Dev)
3. ~~Beeboy's house~~ (Just no. Not for all the fried eggs in a bag of Haribo Starmix)
4. ~~A friend other than Beeboy and Scribs's house~~ (Non-applicable)

5. ~~Homeless shelter~~ (Communal toilets)
6. ~~Travelling circus~~ (Overpowering animal smells)
7. The funhouse

OK, so the funhouse was a whopping twenty-five metres from the bungalow, but it had some positives. Technically, I was upsizing. The funhouse was spread out over three floors. It also came with built-in home surveillance; the thing creaked like mad as soon as you put a big toe on it, so there'd be no fear of being intruded upon in the middle of the night. It didn't have a

TV or wi-fi, but it did have a large red and white spinning disc, a horizontal revolving cylinder and a super-fast crazy slide. There was even a pitch-black corridor with glow-in-the-dark clown faces painted on the ceiling, which I could use for my sleeping quarters.

As soon as I'd arrived home, I set about moving my living essentials down the garden.

Everything I need to move out:
1. Sleeping bag and pillow
2. Three blankets of varying tog values (for temperature control)
3. An extra hoodie
4. Dressing gown
5. Toothbrush
6. Portable stereo (for news updates via radio)
7. A Toblerone (in case of emergencies)

Caroline had left a note on the kitchen counter saying she'd be home a bit later than usual and 'could we talk then?' Apparently, she had extra work to finish off – if that's what swapping saliva round the back of the Pleasure Beach ticket office shed is called these days.

In the solace of my empty bungalow, I chewed on my chicken and chips, swigged a glass of cow juice and banished any nostalgic thoughts into the darkest recesses of my skull.

Once I'd finished, I cleared away my dishes, stacking them beside the sink as I always do for Caroline to wash and put away.

All that was left to do was to put pen to paper.

Caroline,

In light of recent events, I'm writing to inform you that I have decided to leave home to seek out a life in pastures new. While there is no guarantee that they will be any greener, I anticipate that, at the very least, they won't be covered in bull-Snickers.

Leon

P.S. Please note the following points:

1. I will now be living in the funhouse at the end of the garden. While our proximity may tempt you to consider me as a neighbour, please note that I won't tolerate any neighbourly conviviality or attempts from your side to interact with me on these grounds.

2. My breakfast, dinner and tea should be left on the kitchen counter as per the normal routine. Please have the decency to vacate the kitchen for a 20-minute period during the following times: 7.30 a.m., 12.15 p.m. and 8 p.m., so that I can eat without any disturbance.

3. I am reserving the use of the bathroom facilities daily, at the following times: 7–7.30 a.m. (morning wash), 12.40–12.55 p.m. (bowel clearance), 8.20–8.40 p.m. (evening wash).

4. Do not, under any circumstances, tamper with the settings on the Humidex in the bunker or the temperature levels on the air con. If either apparatus should unexpectedly crash, you can alert me via text ONLY using the pre-discussed emergency data info template already saved to your phone and I will take the appropriate measures.

I spent the evening hours settling into my new digs. Sure, it was a tad rickety, a bit on the cold side, but at least now I wouldn't be bothered any more by the gurgling sound of the immersion in the airing cupboard, or the wind whistling through my poorly insulated bedroom windows. And most importantly, I wasn't going to be disturbed by anyone.

I was now a free electron, a lone ranger. A solitary Smartie. And long may it stay that way.

26
Rude Awakenings

'Joseph Rowntree, co-founder of the Rowntree's confectionery company, secured the title trademark for Kit Kat in 1911. Popular myth suggests that the name Kit Kat was an acronym for his wife's former sorority house greeting. What was it?'

'Keep In Touch, Kappa Alpha Theta.'

'Correct. During World War Two, a shortage of milk forced Rowntree's to switch from milk chocolate to dark chocolate in its Kit Kat bars. To signify the change, the company changed the wrapper from red to which colour?'

'Blue.'

'Correct. The now infamous slogan "Have a break, have a Kit-Kat" television ad aired for the first time in which year?'

'1958.'

'Correct. Japan has produced more than two hundred flavours of Kit Kat bars. Part of the appeal stems from Kit Kat's completely unintentional similarity to the Japanese phrase 'Kitto Katsu', which roughly translates as what?'

'"Surely win".'

'Correct. In 2015, a new luxury and giftable variant of the Kit

Kat bar was launched in Malaysia and was made with premium chocolate truffle cream and imported roasted hazelnut pieces. What was its name?'

'Kit Kat Ruby.'

'Correct! Your time is up. No passes, Leon, and with your specialist subject, the history of the Kit Kat bar, you have set a new Mastermind *record—'*

'Psssst…'

'—with an impressive score of—'

'Oi!'

'What, Caroline?' I moaned softly with my gaze still focused on gameshow host John Humphrys applauding my performance, as he does at the end of all my *Mastermind* dreams.

'Oi! Anyone there?'

Intruder.

I sprang into full consciousness and I fumbled out of my sleeping bag, grabbing my dressing gown as I raced up the nearest set of stairs, until I was on the roof of the funhouse.

I looked down.

A man was standing in the middle of the long grass, staring back up at me.

Big.

Burly.

Bald.

Beer-bellied.

Jim.

Yes.

Him.

'All right there, fella?' he said with a smile. 'Remember me? Jim. From the Pleasure Beach. I'm not disturbin', am I?'

'Yes,' I replied.

'Oh, sorry 'bout that. It's just… I wasn't getting an answer from the doorbell, so I thought I'd pop round back to see if anyone was about. I'm looking for yer mam. She in?'

So, it's that low an IQ, is it?

'Well, if she didn't answer the front door, chances are she's not in.'

'Oh right. When d'ya think she'll be back, then?'

'What do I look like, an oracle?' I snapped.

'Come again, son?'

Son… son? I suddenly wanted to reach for a loaded crossbow or a cauldron of boiling molasses.

'Jim! Jim!' Caroline's voice crowed out from the kitchen window. We both looked in her direction as she jogged out the back door barefoot in her dressing gown, with her wet hair tumbling out of a bulky purple head towel.

'Jim! What are you doing round here?' she said when she reached him. 'I was in the shower when you called.'

'I was just dropping off yer work keys; you left 'em in the truck yesterday. I woulda popped 'em through the letterbox but with all the keychains you have on there, they wouldn't fit.'

Caroline stuffed the huge bunch of keys into the pocket of her dressing gown. Then she looked up at me with squinted eyes. 'Morning, lovie. Did you sleep OK last night? It's nippy enough outside.'

'Like a baby,' I quipped. Little did Caroline know that when I said I'd slept like a baby, I'd actually meant a newborn baby who wakes up multiple times in the night crying hysterically for no apparent reason whatsoever.

'Oh, OK. Good,' she said before mouthing to me that she'd read my letter and could we speak about it later?

'No, Caroline, we cannot speak about the letter I wrote you,' I said loudly. 'I've nothing else to say.'

Jim looked at the two of us, completely brain-tied. 'Am I... gettin' in the way of sommink here?'

Well, that's the understatement of the century!

I pointed to the rusty metal frame beneath my feet. 'I live here now. You're both trespassing on my property.'

Caroline's shoulders dropped in disappointment. 'Leon, please can you come down from there so we can talk this out, the two of us?'

'Negative, Caroline. The letter could not have been more explicit. All I want now is to be left alone.'

'Leon! Leon! Tanya, look! It's Leon! He's on the roof of the funhouse. Leon! Leon!'

Oh great, things were about to go from bad to Beeboy. God? Yoda? E.T.? Somebody just throw down a death ray or a piece of space debris and put me out of my misery.

'All right, mate?' said Scribs as she and Beeboy waded their way through the dense foliage. 'We knocked on your front door, but nobody was answering.'

'Hello,' said Caroline, waving at Scribs and Beeboy even though they were now standing only a few metres from them. 'I'm Caroline, Leon's mum, and this is Jim.'

'Oh, yeah, from the Pleasure Beach, right?' Scribs said.

'Yes, that's right… we didn't get a chance to properly speak the last time we—'

'Caroline, in my letter I *specifically* stated that any neighbourly conviviality or attempts from your side to interact with me on such grounds would *not* be tolerated.'

'I was just saying hello, Leon,' Caroline said quietly. 'That's hardly a crime now, is it?'

'True, Caroline, there are worse things to be accused of… betrayal for example…'

Scribs scrambled to ease the tension. 'Eh, we just wanted to stop by on our break and check up on you, mate. You didn't tell us you weren't coming to school today.'

Jim looked back up at me. 'Yeah, there's a thought and all. Why you not in school today, son?'

OK, that's it. From now on I'm going to keep a stock of well-sharpened harpoons on the roof *at all times*.

I glared back down at him. 'Why are *you* still here?'

'Best be off…' Scribs mumbled.

'We're not leaving *already*, are we?' whined Beeboy. 'We didn't even get to show Leon the do-up plans for the funhouse we worked on.'

'Can I take a look?' Jim asked. 'I'm a handyman by trade. Can do a bit of everything. I could give your plans the once-over if you like?'

Scribs went to hand over the rolled-up poster card she had tucked under her arm.

'*Don't* even think about it!' I roared. 'Those plans are strictly confidential. You can leave them on the bottom step.'

'OK,' Scribs said awkwardly. 'Take a look when you've chilled a bit and get back to me, K?'

'Come back to school soon, Leon! We miss you!' Beeboy called as Scribs dragged him back through the grass.

Caroline waited until the two of them had disappeared from sight, then folded her arms and stared up at me with a *not cool, Leon* face.

'Leon, please come down from there.'

'No.'

'Leon—'

'I said no, Caroline. Final answer.'

She lowered her head and started to make her way back up the garden. 'Come on, Jim. I'll make us some tea.'

I looked down at Jim and smiled proudly.

Jim smoothed his moustache with his fingers. 'You really are sommink else, aren't ya? That doctor was right and all about you being as rigid as a bargepole.'

What did he just say?

'Can't be helped, of course,' he continued. 'It's that brain condition, you've got, isn't it? God bless ya, son.'

He turned and made his way back up the garden to join Caroline in the kitchen, while I clenched my fists until they looked like red, puffy boxing mitts.

27
Snot what you think

'Leon John Crothers to see Dr Snot.'

'Well, well, Carol, look who we have here.'

So, there's two of them now, is there?

'Carol is such a typical receptionist's name. That and Trish. I bet *your* name's Trish. It's Trish, isn't it?'

'How d'you know that? Carol, you hearing this?'

'I really don't have time to go into the specifics, Trish. Thank God,' I answered back as I walked over to the doc's office.

'Don't even *think* about going in there! Mouthy little brat. Carol, have you ever heard such cheek in all yer life?'

The doc was startled when I burst in. 'Leon!'

'Doc.'

'What are you doing here?'

'I thought I'd drop by so I could condemn you to hell, along with your loved ones, friends, household pets, etc.'

The doc looked back at me, stunned. 'Leon, I'm just about to receive a patient. Now's *really* not the—'

'How's working out at the gym been working out for you?' I gave him the once-over. 'Not a bit of difference, clearly. At least it correlates well with the absolute truth.'

'Leon—'

'So, you've been introduced to *Jim*… or "one in a gazillion" Jim, as Caroline calls him.'

'Leon—'

'It *also* transpires that I've got a problem with rigidity – a comment that has *clearly* come from your manipulative influence. You openly discussed my file with Caroline and Jim in the cosy autumn sunshine, spreading false allegations nonetheless!'

'Now, now, Leon, why don't you just take a moment to calm down,' the doc urged.

I gripped the edge of his desk. 'Listen carefully, Snotface. I'm no more rigid than a Twizzler.'

'A Twizzler?'

'Yes, a twenty-centimetre-long strawberry-flavoured liquorice-type candy, manufactured by Y&S Candies Inc., of Lancaster, Pennsylvania. Its ingredients consist of corn syrup, wheat flour, sugar, cornstarch and, in smaller amounts, palm oil, salt, artificial flavour, glycerine, citric acid, potassium sorbate, Red 40 and soy lecithin.'

I took my rucksack off my back, unzipped it, held it upside down and shook a kilo of Twizzlers onto the doc's desk.

'Even *you* should be able to gather from the sum-up of its components, Doc, that a Twizzler is in fact as flaccid as a—'

'Now, just… hold your horses there, Leon.'

'What horses?'

'"Hold your horses" is an idiom for "stop right there", Leon.'

'Then why don't you just say that, then? Why the hell bring horses into it? And *no*, I *won't* stop right there. You need to understand the gravity of the situation! You spoke about *my* personal medical records to a total stranger! That's illegal!'

'Leon, when I bumped into your mother and her partner, Jim, we only spoke about the good weather and the how the roadworks on Market Street were dragging far longer than expected. That was it. Your file wasn't even mentioned.'

'Then why did Jim say to me in his common as muck cockney accent, "That doctor was right and all about you being rigid as a bargepole. Can't be helped, of course, it's that brain condition you've got."'

The doc winced uncomfortably. 'Well, it may have been the case that Caroline spoke to Jim about your condition. Which isn't illegal, I'm afraid.'

As if!

'Caroline wouldn't do a thing like that. Telling me off for saying that elderly ladies look like penguins because they waddle and smell like fish, when I'm standing right behind one in the street, yes, but *not* that.'

'You know, Leon, people with autism often depend highly on routine and ritual. To shift the pieces of the puzzle *can* cause great frustration and anxiety. But, believe me, there are many coping mechanisms that can be put in place to help deal with this rigidity.'

I grabbed a Twizzler from the desk and twisted the red liquorice rope into a knot. 'For the last time... I am *not* rigid! See? See that?!'

'What about your mealtime schedule, Leon? Would you not say that that's a form of rigidity?'

'Oh, for God's sake... so now we have to label meal preferences as a symptom of crazy man's syndrome?'

'Well, answer me this: how would you feel if this evening you had to eat something different to what you're accustomed to eating? A salad, for example.'

My elbows began to itch. 'Fine by me, Doc. Why would I have a problem with that?'

'Because you require things to always be on your terms. You don't cope well with change.'

Anger. Frustration. Anger.

'Yes, I do. I've moved schools *six* times. Aha! So there!'

'But the very fact that you keep moving schools is because you can't tolerate these environments, Leon. You struggle to accept that in school you have to conform to an established set of rules and guidelines, just like the other students.'

Rage now bordering on a desire to demonstrate aggression.

'As your doctor, Leon, I would highly recommend that you—'

I pounded on the doc's desk with my fists. 'As of *right* now, you're under strict instructions to remove any noticeable trace of my name and personal information from your records. Your presumed diagnosis is completely false, which thereby makes you a fraud. A *fraud*! This is an even greater scandal than the time US food corporation Kraft launched a bilateral attack on a British institution in 2015 and changed the recipe of Cadbury's Creme Eggs by switching out Dairy Milk for a 'standard cocoa mix chocolate' in the shell *and* reducing their number in boxes from six to five!'

With one clean sweep, I sent the pile of Twizzlers crashing into a wall, before storming out of the doc's office, down the hall and out the automatic doors. If only Glen had been waiting for me in the car park when I'd come out. I had so much anger surging inside me, I'm pretty sure I could have rearranged his smug-looking face and strung him up on a lamp post.

A sort of sorry consolation prize.

28
Choices

In case the thought hadn't crossed your mind, writing a book is a tedious, exhausting, torturous thing to do.

Oh yeah, it's easy for you to sit back in your cosy sun-lounger or hospital bed or jail cell and flitter along from chapter to chapter. Did you ever consider the fact that every single word that is typed onto these pages was hemmed and hawed over for many sleepless nights and dragged through ferocious wars of words with literary agents, editors, publishers, etc.?

So why bother to write a book, then? I hear you say.

Well, it's not for the money, that's for sure. By the end of all this, I'll be lucky if I have enough to pay for a haircut and a bus ticket.

Control. The answer is control.

When you write a story, you decide what happens: who wins or loses, who lives or dies. *You* have the control. Even if the 'back office' production teams want to exercise their power of authority, ultimately, *you* have the last word. Because without the writer, there is no story.

Control. It's all about the control.

OK, so maybe this is me saying that I might have, as it turns out, a slight lack of flexibility in my nature. It's true that I'll only use Quilted Velvet toilet paper and no other brand. Yes, I do make a fuss when Caroline lets the temperature in the house surpass 19 degrees, even on rare occasions when it snows. Sure, I refuse to eat in the kitchen when the dishwasher's on because the humming noise interrupts me chewing my food to the rhythm of the Canadian national anthem. But, honestly, what's the big deal? These are just impassioned lifestyle choices. They hardly define me as being a control freak, do they?

It only took a quarter hour of walking around the car park outside the doc's office for me to figure all this out.

The trouble was, I was still angry.

Angry and alone.

I suddenly got an overwhelming urge to see Scribs.

Twenty minutes later, I was knocking on her front door.

A middle-aged woman I'd never seen before, who was wearing a nurse's uniform, answered.

'Is she in?' I asked.

'Eh, which "she" are you looking for?' the woman wanted to know.

'Well not the busty five-foot-eleven one with a voice like a scrambler bike, that's for sure,' I answered.

'Ah, so it's Tanya you want, then.'

'How'd you guess that so quick?'

'Well, I only have two daughters.'

'Really? How many sons do you have?'

'None.'

'Two kids, is that all? That's unusual for where you live.'

'I'm guessing *you* must be Leon.' She chuckled. 'Tanya talks a lot about you.'

'I'd discredit most of what you've been told. She's dyslexic, so she's prone to inaccuracies.'

'Well, from what I've heard so far, she's got you spot on,' she said, now laughing away to herself. A genuine, hearty laugh.

Scribs appeared at the door.

'Honestly, Tanya! What took you so long to walk the whole six metres from your bedroom?' I said, half exasperated.

'Sor-ry. I had to use the bog.'

'Can I come in?'

'Sure,' the woman said, swinging the door open wide. 'I'm Donna. Delighted to finally meet you, Leon.'

Delighted to meet me? *Me*? Leon John Crothers? The kid with the attitude problem? This couldn't be right.

'What's your hidden agenda?' I asked her.

'Beg your pardon?'

'I'm confused. Most people are delighted to see the back of me. I tend to anger, offend or upset easily.'

'Mum's a senior nurse at The Harbour mental health hospital,' Scribs said. 'Nothing fazes her. Trust me.'

'So that explains it,' I said, speaking to Donna. 'You've clearly heard a lot more cuckoo than anything that'll come out of my mouth.'

'Oh yeah, including a patient I looked after some years back who used to run around the wards crying out "cuckoo" every hour on the hour.' She reached into the bottom of her handbag and pulled out her keys. 'Right, Tans, I'm off. There's leftover stir-fry in the fridge. Should be enough for you and Denise. Dev told me he'd grab something to eat on the way home. Try to get to bed early, I'll be in late.'

She put a hand on my shoulder, which I was uncomfortable with but not entirely disgusted by. 'Sorry to have to rush off. I hope you'll come round again, Leon, when I'm in, so we can have a cuppa and a chat. Tanya's told me you're very interesting to listen to.'

I shook my head. 'No thanks, Donna. Tanya's right in saying that I'm interesting to listen to, but to be very honest, I'm not much of a conversationalist. I bore quickly of people's generic small talk.'

'Oh yeah?' Scribs butted in. 'So, I'm guessing you wouldn't wanna know about how Mum here's a former British champion for eating M&Ms?'

Eh, come again?

I side-stepped Donna and blocked her passage to the front door.

'I'm sorry, but you can't leave here without providing answers to the following questions: Who? What? Where? When? Why? What?'

Donna tried to speak seriously through a massive grin. 'Yours truly. M&Ms speed-eating competition. NHS Blackpool charity fundraiser for mental health unit resources. 1996. Because I'm jolly good at eating M&Ms.'

'And?'

'*And*?'

'I said "Who? What? Where? When? Why? What?" You didn't answer the second "what".'

'What was the second "what" for?'

I groaned impatiently. 'Your score! What was your score?'

'Oh, right! Sixty-one M&Ms in sixty seconds.'

My face dropped. 'That's an absolutely *woeful* score. No, worse than that, it's downright abysmal. There are YouTube videos of university students averaging scores of well over a hundred. And you go around advertising that? That's ballsy.'

'Did I mention that the competition was how many M&Ms a person could eat in one minute using chopsticks...?'

Holy Snickers.

'Are you aware that the current Guinness World Record for the most M&Ms eaten in one minute using chopsticks is sixty-five and was achieved by Kathryn Ratcliffe from the UK on a live TV programme in Beijing, China, on the eighteenth of August 2011? That's only *four* less than her score.'

'Is it really? Blimey! Maybe I should get myself into shape then... get a training programme together... reach for the big time.'

'Donna, I'd happily offer to coach you, except my hand-eye coordination isn't far off that of an octopus's. I could, however, source you a supply of M&Ms to practise with. Ones that are perhaps a good nine months or so past their sell-by-date? Meaning their candy shell coating would have less of a sheen, which could definitely assist in the rapidity of picking them up with chopsticks.'

'Thanks for that, Leon. We'll chat about it again when I'm between shifts, OK?'

She coaxed me to the side of the door and waved to us both as she slipped out the door with a smile like an upside-down rainbow.

I liked this Donna lady. Very much.

Scribs collapsed onto the sofa in peals of laughter. 'You're hilarious! Proper hilarious!'

I flopped down beside her. 'And you are an out-and-out sneak… imagine not telling me a thing like that after all the time we've known each other?'

'What… two whole weeks?' she said while tousling my hair, something she's grown accustomed to doing when she's teasing me and which I don't incredibly dislike.

'So… what's got you calling round here outta nowhere? Who'd ya catch kissing who this time?'

'My doctor,' I answered.

'Yer doctor?!'

'Yep. Kissing his practitioner's license goodbye. You don't

happen to have a good contact for a lawyer, do you? One that has experience in medical law? Or possibly fraud? Slander?'

'Nah. FYI, I've got homework that needs getting done, so why don't you just tell me in plain old En-ger-lish what's up?'

'On a scale of one to ten (one being the lowest, ten being the highest), how rigid would you say I am?'

Scribs thought for a moment. 'I'd have to say three.'

'Three? Really? Is that all?'

'Yeah, three. Million. Three million out of ten. Noel, you're so rigid that it shocks me how you'd even be ok with that spelling rule about the I before e, or e before c, or, hang on, what's the—'

'I before e, except after c, Scribs…'

'That's the one. So why you asking me that anyway?'

'Well… if I'm that rigid, then how are you even OK with speaking to me on a more or less daily basis?'

'Dunno. Yeah, maybe you're right, I should kick your bony arse outta here pronto…' She stuck out her tongue, which was grazed and whitish down the centre… hmm… just what had she been snacking on?

'What are you staring at? You're wondering if I've been eating sweets, aren't ya?'

'It's blatantly obvious you've been eating sweets, Scribs. I'm gonna guess a quarter bag of Tangfastics?'

'Oh my God, Noel, you're magic! How'd you even know that I've been… you see, *that's* why I hang out with you: you're different. You're a *complete* misfit and you don't give a toss. I love that. Even more than jazzies.'

Wow. I wasn't expecting that. Suddenly the microscopic hairs on the backs of my calves were bristling.

'Yeah, but the rigid thing. That's a problem, isn't it?'

'For me? Not really. Annoying at times, sure. But so what? We've all got good and bad bits, right? If like, say I stopped at the fact that you can be a bit of a control freak, then I wouldn't get to hear all the hilarious gems that you come out with. So, I just work round it.'

'That's easy for you, Scribs. You're not rigid. Your brain allows you to bend and buckle around these kinds of situations. Mine can't. Especially with this whole Caroline and Jim crisis. It's impossible!'

'Did your brain tell you that?' she said. 'Or are you just spinning excuses?'

No comment.

She then moved herself up closer to me on the sofa, close enough that I could smell her breath. The last Tangfastic she'd eaten before coming out here was a fizzy cola bottle. No doubt.

'You like your mum, yeah?'

'Well—'

'Ah ah ah... not an actual question, mate.'

When *will* she grasp the concept of the question mark?

'Deep down, you know your mum's an important person in your life. If she wasn't, then you wouldn't be so miffed about her having a fella, now would ya? So, if you really like your mum, and she really likes this Jim bloke, then maybe there's things about him that you could like too?'

'But—' I tried to insist.

She pushed her fingers onto my lips and held them there. 'D'you know what, Noel? I'm *sure* there's things about Jim that aren't that bad. Sure, he'll have his annoying bits, like the rest of us, but guess what, you treating him like a piece of dirt before even getting to know him? That's not very smart. It's proper stupid. And you're not big on "stupid people" last time I checked, are you?'

I shook my head slowly.

She took her fingers off my mouth. 'Go home, Noel. *Home* home. Give 'em both a chance. Tomorrow's Saturday, yeah? Beeboy and me will drop round in the morning to hang out a bit, look over the funhouse plans, etc. and we'll take the temperature of the situation, OK? But give it a real chance, yeah? Don't be rigid. Be non-rigid.'

'Non-rigid isn't a word.'

'Whatever! Be open-minded. I bet you this time tomorrow, you'll be saying that it wasn't half as bad as you were making the whole thing out to be in your head.'

I sensed that this was my cue to get up off the sofa and head towards the door.

'That's a mammoth ask, Scribs. I'm going to have to think about it. That and where I could get my hands on recently expired M&Ms. Maybe Poundland.'

'Betcha Jim could help you with that. He seems like the type with friends in dodgy places…'

'Eh, Scribs, didn't you say you'd got homework to finish? Go back to forgetting your i's and inverting your t's.'

She playfully fired a cushion at me from the sofa, as I slid out the door.

'Get lost, cheeky brat!'

Blue skies greeted me when I walked away from Bethany Crescent. They stuck around for my entire walk home, a definite bonus. Don't go thinking that I'm mentioning this weather detail to draw up a sappy metaphor to suggest that my head was now filled with sunbeams and rainbows.

I still felt angry, *really* angry.

But I did have a plan, which meant I had hope.

Well, a little, at least.

How *does* she do it?

29
Rigid? Me?

I'm not rigid. I'm not rigid.

I'm a Twizzler.

Flexible, bendable, wriggly, jiggly.

All I have to do is ring the doorbell.

I'm a Twizzler. I'm a Twizzler.

'Leon?'

'Caroline.'

Her face was all smiles. 'Well, you're the last person I was expecting to see at the front door!'

Itchy elbows, dry eyelids, a surge in blood pressure.

I'm a Twizzler. I'm a Twizzler.

'I… I just wanted to ask about my tea.'

'Your tea? But it's only 6 p.m., lovie.'

Come on. Say it. Say it. Just say it.

'I, eh…'

Twizzler. I'm a Twizzler.

'Could… could… I have my tea here with you this evening?'

Huh. That wasn't so bad.

Caroline's smile then went a bit lopsided. 'Well, I'd actually made plans to eat out this evening. Respecting the terms and conditions of your letter, I thought that if I ate out, you'd have a bit more time in the kitchen by yourself. That is what you want, isn't it?'

Aargh! Of course that's not what I want. I want things to go back to the way they were! Me and Caroline. Caroline and me. I want us to be sitting at our table, eating our tea, together. Me with my chips well distanced from my sausages and Caroline's trademark mountain of salt that she piles up on the edge of her plate and uses as a dipping station. Normal. I want things to be normal. Why can't I tell her that? Why is it so hard to tell her that?

Caroline was trying to decode my blinks and twitches while I was hashing all this out in my head.

'D'you know what, Leon, why don't I cancel my plans and we'll eat together, just the two of us?'

Ah! That's more like it. What a relief!

'OK, fine,' I said. 'So long as the mealtime manifesto is respected.'

'Sure,' she said, opening the door wider to let me pass. 'Though I must say I thought you'd be all fired up to discuss this morning's headlines.'

'What headlines?'

'Didn't you see the *Sun* article I taped to the front of the funhouse for you this morning? John Humphrys is retiring from *Mastermind* at the end of the year. Clive Myrie's replacing him.'

Is she taking the Pez?

There's no way that can be true.

'John Humphrys is retiring from *Mastermind*?! What kind of a sordid hoax is that?'

'I'm pretty sure it isn't a hoax, Leon. Afterall, Humphrys has been getting on a bit…'

'And they're bringing in Clive Myrie? From *News at Ten*? Which bigwig at the BBC decided that?!'

Deep breaths, Crothers. Deep breaths. You knew this day would come. It's the end of an era, that's all it is. The end of an era.

'So, sausage and chips, tonight, Leon. Will it be two sausages as usual?' Caroline asked.

'Three sausages, Caroline, I've barely eaten all day. Also, make sure the crinkle cuts are crisped up good and proper, as they should be.'

She stood to attention and made a dramatic military salute. 'I'm just going call Jim and tell him there's been a change of plan. Then I'll crack on with tea .'

I thought I was in the clear, but then the weirdest thing happened.

Scribs appeared.

Out of nowhere.

No, not at my front door… in my *head*. I could hear her mooching around my subconscious as if she was on the hunt for a sugary snack.

'All right, mate? What you up to?'

'What do you mean, what am I up to, Scribs? You're the one rifling around my inner thoughts – get out!'

'Rifling? What you on about? Do I look like someone who goes around trying to shoot people?'

'Don't even think about pilfering any of my linguistic capabilities, Scribs, not a single past pronoun, is that clear?'

'Let's get on with things before your mum thinks you've gone mad. Why you being so rigid?'

'Rigid? I've just conceded to having my tea with Caroline, in spite of the fact that I'm still furious with her!'

'Nice try, mate, I saw the little pretend victory dance you were doing in here when she said she'd change her plans. Why don't you tell her to invite Jim round for tea?'

'What? Are you insane?!'

'Didn't you say you were gonna give the two of 'em a chance?'

'No! That was you! I never agreed to anything!'

'Oh yeah, well, guess what, you're the one imagining all of this right now… your gut's trying to tell you something.'

'Yes, that I'm hungry. Very, very hungry.'

'Well then, better let you get on with doing the right thing, so…'

'Scribs! Wait! Come back! Scribs!'

'Leon? … Leon?'

Caroline's voice startled me.

'Leon, are you OK? You'd completely zoned out for a

moment there.'

'Eh, yes. Fine. I'm fine.'

Twizzler. I'm a Twizzler. A Twizzler.

'Caroline… you… you…'

'Yes, lovie?'

Come on, mate, you're a Twizzler, yeah? Do the tight ring… sorry… the right thing…

'You… eh… Jim… could come eat… with us…'

Caroline looked at me in astonishment. 'Really, Leon? Do you mean that?'

No.

'…OK…'

Her face lit up. 'That would be great! Look, I know things have gotten off to a rocky start with Jim, but he's honestly a really good person, trust me. And he's really keen to get to know you better.'

Then came the *really* horrific bit. She leant forward and gave me an unrequested hug. It took every fibre of my being not to shove her off me. I *hate* hugs with a passion. Caroline knows that. She hasn't dared hug me since that time on the promenade back when I was six and I screamed at the top of my lungs that I was being abducted to get her to stop. I remember she was a bit moody for a while after that, especially after we'd been allowed to leave the police station.

'Bunker! I've got to go to my bunker!' I said as I broke free.

30
Only Smarties Have
the Answer

Everything you need to know about my bunker:

1. Its temperature is regulated at 18.3 degrees Celsius
2. My worktable is made of white granite and cost me three years' worth of Christmas presents
3. My sweet stash samples are stored in individual Pyrex tool part drawers and arranged alphabetically
4. The storage units are dusted once a week
5. The bunker is a no-smoking, no-sneezing, no-coughing, no-burping, no-farting area
6. The spare key is hidden in the bottom of our sugar bowl in the kitchen

I'd be lying if I said that it wasn't a moment of profound joy to be reacquainted with my bunker. You see, while the bungalow is technically my dwelling (is/was, whatever), my bunker is my refuge from the world. Everything in it has its place and everything has its purpose. It is a shrine to my work and it contains within its walls not just my sacred sweet stash, but my hopes and dreams.

So, you can imagine how annoyed I was when I heard a loud banging on my triple-reinforced door only forty-eight minutes after I'd settled in.

I scanned my desk clock. 7.08 p.m.

'No, Caroline, I don't plan to wash before tea!' I shouted in the direction of the door. 'But, if you're going to use the shower, *do not*, I repeat, *do not* move the used cotton bud I've left leaning up by the soap dish. I hit the jackpot yesterday and want to inspect it one last time before getting rid of it!'

The metal door suddenly swung open.

'All right, son? Mind if I come in?'

You're *kidding* me.

Why has he shown up so early? Food won't be ready for at least another half hour. What was Caroline thinking, letting him wander down here? And no, it's not OK to just 'come in'. Doesn't he know that this bunker is the confectionery equivalent of Area 51?

'Now's not a good time,' I said, as I continued to empty the contents of a tube of Smarties onto my worktable with long surgical tweezers.

But instead of exercising some form of polite obedience, he just walked on in, as if I'd said, 'Sure thing, mate, make yourself at home.'

'Yer mam said it was your idea that I pop round for tea. Cheers for that.'

He approached my worktable. 'What's going on over here, then?'

I could see visible moisture on his hands. Was it sweat? Or mucus from a messy sneeze? Or had he just been in the bathroom and had drizzled a bit of tap water over his palms after a 'big job' on the loo? Ugh! He's a fully-fledged bacteria trafficker!

I held up a latex-gloved hand and signalled him to keep back.

'I'm conducting a quantity and colour variety control check across a selected sample of Smarties tubes. Normally, the average tube contains thirty-five Smarties, but recent internet rumours have been suggesting that this figure has been quietly reduced to thirty-three, so I'm looking into it.'

'Oh, right,' he said, backing away slightly.

The lightbulb above our heads then started flickering. It immediately caught Jim's attention.

'Looks like you've got a knackered bulb there, son.'

'The lightbulb's fine,' I told him. 'It's the wiring that's knackered, but it's OK, I'm used to it.'

'Used to it? How can you work under that? Your bulb's playing around like a strobe light in a disco!'

'I've trained my eyes to blink in synchronisation with the flickering,' I explained. 'And it doesn't flicker all the time. Only when Caroline's got the fat-fryer on full blast. If anything, it's an indication that she's on time with meal preparations.'

'I can take a look at that wiring for ya if ya like?' Jim said, examining the bulb. 'I dabble a bit with electrics.'

And risk interferences with my air-con thermostat? Who does he take me for? A kamikaze?

'Not necessary,' I replied.

He then gave up staring at the ceiling and pointed to a large photograph that was mounted on the wall.

'That your grandad?' he asked.

'Pfff... I wish,' I said, as I carried on with my work. 'That's H.B. Reese.'

'Who?'

I sighed.

'H.B. Reese – Harry Burnett Reese. He invented the Reese's Peanut Butter Cup (a chocolate disc filled with a peanut butter mixture) in the basement of his house in 1928. Today it's the US's leading confectionery brand. Over two billion dollars in sales per year.'

'Did you say two billion quid a year?!' said Jim, now sussing out the photo up close, 'I can't believe that!'

'Neither can I at times. The filling inside those things tastes like moist sand, but that's America for you.'

Jim then crossed the room and started eyeing up my stash. 'Incredible... I mean, yer mam did tell me yer mad for sweets and the like, but I gotta admit I was *not* expecting this.'

I could sense that Jim's fingers were itching to wrench open some of the drawers. That made me uncomfortable, which made me nervous, which made my left hand jerk suddenly and knock over a tube of Smarties. They scattered everywhere. Half of them ended up on the floor.

Fudge.

'Here, lemme help you with those,' said Jim, and he bent down to scoop them up with his moist hands.

I held out a waste-paper basket in his direction.

'You're not seriously gonna chuck 'em, are ya?' he said. 'Ever heard of the old five-second rule?' He laughed.

I didn't.

When he realised I was deadly serious about disposing of the spoilt goods, he shovelled a handful of the things into his mouth.

'So, what's there to know about these things, then?' he asked.

'What? Smarties?'

'Yeah.'

'A lot of things.'

'Go on then.'

'Why?'

'Cuz I'm interested.'

Interested? Oh, *I* get it. This is all part of some ambitious strategy he has to win me over. As if I couldn't see that one coming a mile off. He thinks that by faking an interest in *my* interest, I'll turn a blind eye to the fact that he's snogging Caroline.

Well, if that's his game plan, then I was about to announce *game over*.

'Jim…' I said to the whites of his eyes. 'Smarties are colour-varied, sugar-coated, chocolate oblate spheroids, manufactured since 1937, originally by H.I. Rowntree & Company in the UK, and are currently produced by Nestlé. They are sold across Europe, in particular Northern and Central Europe, as well as Canada, South Africa, Australasia and the Middle East. Smarties are not distributed in the United States, where the rights to the name belong to the Smarties Candy Company, which manufactures its own hard tablet sweet under the registered trademark name Smarties. The original Smarties colours were dark brown, light brown, green, orange, pink, violet and yellow. Milk chocolate was used as the inner flavouring for all original Smarties, except the light brown ones, which were coffee-flavoured up until 1958, when the flavouring was removed. Orange-flavoured Smarties can only be found in Smarties manufactured for the UK market. Originally the milk chocolate itself was flavoured with orange essence, but now orange flavouring is only added to the sugar shell. Today, Smarties come in eight colours: red, orange, yellow, green, blue, mauve, pink and brown. The blue Smartie replaced the light brown Smartie in 1988 and was originally introduced to oppose the planned takeover of Rowntree Mackintosh Confectionery Company by Nestlé, during which time pin badges with the phrase "I support Blue

Smarties" were circulated. In 2006, however, blue Smarties were axed amid health fears over the chemical agent used in the blue colouring (Brilliant Blue FD&C, Blue 7, E133), and were replaced with white Smarties while Nestlé researched an alternative colourant. Blue Smarties were finally reintroduced in 2008, using dye from the cyanobacterium spirulina, a natural colouring derived from seaweed.'

Wait…

Damn it!

Brain! What are you playing at? Since when is it OK to leave the controls on autopilot?

Caroline's voice suddenly rang out from overhead.

'Tea's on the table!'

'Lovely jubbvely!' Jim hollered back. He reached out and gave me a strong pat on the back that nearly toppled me forwards. 'Brilliant! That's proper impressive, son. You've got a real talent there!'

Now should have been the perfect moment to recuperate from my Smarties monologue mishap and tell Jim that he has a real talent for tearing wholesome families apart or spreading germs around a room faster than spreading cream cheese on a bagel, or something like that, but instead I blurted out, 'Really?'

Really? *Really? Where* did that come from? Nobody needs to tell me that I'm a penny-sweet prodigy. *Of course* I've got talent. I've got tuck-shop-loads of talent! Caroline's even jokingly told me off in the past for overdoing it on the ego-tripping, reminding me that 'self-praise is no praise, Leon', not that I could give a fudge.

'One hundred per cent,' he said with a friendly smile as he made his way back upstairs.

I shook my head in disbelief as I looked down at the Smarties on my worktable.

Even they didn't have the answer.

31
HELL

The three of us were piled around the small wooden table in our poky kitchen. Jim's presence made things crowded and uncomfortable: an extra chair, an extra set of elbows on the table, an extra set of cutlery, an extra glass for his can of lager.

And don't even get me started on all the extra noises. There was more sipping, more chewing, more swallowing, more knife-and-fork chinking, more chair creaking... it was stressful. Very, very stressful.

But the baked beans were by *far* the most difficult thing to cope with. Of course, Caroline knew better than to serve me any, but that didn't stop me having to listen to her and Jim wolf down their portions with no qualms whatsoever. The sound coming from their mouths was deafening; they may as well have been slurping the things directly out of my ears.

'Is everything OK, lovie?' Caroline asked when she noticed that I hadn't touched my food.

'Yes,' I mumbled under my breath as I moved my knife and fork around my plate, doing everything possible to camouflage my absolute disgust.

'Are you sure? You're not saying much.'

'I'm… fine.'

'Are you still bothered about Humphrys leaving *Mastermind*? I'm sure Clive will do a great job. He certainly reads the news very well.'

'What's this youse are talkin' about?' asked Jim, with a mouth full of baked beans. Never had I heard anything so foul.

'Leon's a huge fan of the game show *Mastermind* on BBC Two,' Caroline carried on.

'Can't say I've heard of it,' he said as he continued to chew between words.

I could feel a short stream of vomit trying to climb up the back of my throat.

'Oh, really? Leon, why don't you explain the show to Jim? You're the expert, after all.'

I'm a Twizzler, I'm a Twizzler, a Twizzler being stretched to within an inch of its life.

'Why beans? *Why*? What are they, some sort of handyman's dietary requirement?'

Jim and Caroline lowered their knives and forks and stared at me.

Uh-oh.

I raised my hand slightly off the table to gesture a silent apology as I lowered my head and closed my eyes.

Keep it together, Crothers. Keep it together. Just eat quickly and then you can escape.

'All right, mate?'

'What the? Scribs? You again?'

'What's all this about escaping?'

'Now's not the time for wisecracks, Scribs. I'm caught up in the equivalent of a terrorist attack.'

'Terrorist attack? You're just eating your tea, that's all.'

'Jim being here, it's thrown everything off kilter. He's brought the enemy with him.'

'Enemy? You're not on about the baked beans, are ya?'

'Scribs, baked beans are the spawn of Satan. They look like tomato-soaked rats' kidneys and don't get me started on the smell. I shudder to even think what they taste like.'

'You telling me that you've never eaten a baked bean before? You should give 'em a try some time, mate – they're proper yum. I eat 'em with toast. I love it when the bread goes all soft and soggy and you can—'

'Have you shown up to help me or taunt me?'

'Oh yeah, right, sorry. Look, I know it's hard, but that doesn't mean you can't do it. Just try and get a chip on your fork and put it in your gob. It'll get easier then, you'll see. Come on, mate, you're not gonna be defeated by a baked bean, are ya?'

'It's not just the baked beans, Scribs. My senses are being invaded from all sides! If it's not the peppery odour of Jim's cheap cologne that's pinching my nose, it's his incessant throat-clearing that's grating on my eardrums, and don't get me started about the squeaking noise his bum cheeks make *when he fidgets in his chair!'*

'OK, OK, Noel, take a second and chillax, K? Just keep telling yourself that you can do this.'

'Scribs, I can't do this. It's too hard. Why is this so hard?!'

'Yes, you can. I know you can! And don't forget, whatever happens, I'll be round your place tomorrow with Beeboy to check up on you. Stay strong.'

'Anyone for seconds?' Caroline asked.

I zoned back in just in time to reply with a shaky 'no'.

'I wouldn't mind some, thanks,' Jim said, slowly massaging his gut. 'You wouldn't happen to have some brown sauce hanging about the cupboard, would ya?'

'Hmm… I'll have a look,' said Caroline as she stood on her tiptoes to reach for the handle of the cupboard over the fridge.

Brown sauce. The condiment that smells of liquidised cow entrails. Oh, please let there not be any in the cupboard. Please, I beg you.

'Well, look what we have here!'

Snickers. Fudge. Snickers.

'Gosh, first the baked beans and now the brown sauce… this is definitely your lucky night,' Caroline said to Jim playfully as she passed him over a half-empty bottle of HP.

'Cheers, love,' said Jim. He held the glass bottle upside down over his plate and began thumping it sharply with the palm of his hand. Nothing happened at first, then suddenly a huge dollop of brown sludge shot out of the bottle and splashed onto his sausages. Flecks of the stuff landed on the rim of my plate.

'Wow! Sorry 'bout that!'

I'm guessing that's what he said, but I wasn't listening. I was just staring in horror at the spatters of sauce, just millimetres from my crinkle cuts. My itchy elbows were now burning. Then, a large, moist, hairy hand holding a chip stretched over to my plate and wiped up the brown droplets in one clean sweep.

I jerked my head around to look at Jim, who saluted me with his chip.

'Problem solved,' he said with a wink.

Caroline reacted quickly. 'It's all right, Leon, I'll cook you a fresh batch, won't take long.'

She trotted round the table to the fryer.

Jim looked completely flummoxed. 'You're not gonna cook him more chips because of that now, are ya?'

'Oh, it's fine, Jim,' Caroline reassured him.

'You've been rushed off your feet all day at work. You should be taking it easy.'

'It's no trouble at all, promise.'

'But, but the stuff didn't even touch 'em!' Jim continued. 'Doesn't make sense.'

'It doesn't *need* to make sense to you!' I snapped, springing up from the table. 'And for the record, Caroline rides roller coasters for a living. She spends most of her workdays *upside down*.'

They both spun round and stared at me.

Suddenly, I could hear the sound of my racing heartbeat. My mouth was as dry as a cracker.

'Ss… sorry… I… have to go… lie down…'

Caroline nodded her head consolingly.

I forwent all my pre-bedtime routines and headed straight to my room, where I flopped down onto my springy mattress, mentally and emotionally exhausted.

But despite my overwhelming fatigue, I struggled to put myself to sleep; the noise of Caroline and Jim's enthusiastic banter that carried on throughout the evening two rooms over made it an impossible task. What could be so interesting that they'd need to be talking that loudly? And why so much laughter?

With my eyes closed, I tried to remember what Scribs had told me.

Focus on the good bits. All I had to do was focus on the good bits.

He did make her happy. There was no denying it. Jim made Caroline happy.

Though that wasn't so much a good thing as an inconvenient truth.

32
Climate Change

The next morning, the veins on my temples throbbed to Caroline whistling the intro to *Good Morning Britain*. It was an excruciating start to the day. I'd gone to sleep on an empty stomach and had spent a long night drifting in and out of sleep, with my gut calling out to my subconscious for a bunch of bananas, or a carton of milk or a plate of crinkle-cut chips, uniformly cooked, well-rested in kitchen roll just after their quick dip in the fryer, not a drop of brown sauce in sight.

My nose suddenly picked up an aroma of breakfast. I leapt straight from my covers and dashed down the hall in my boxers and my *You wanna piece of me?* Yorkie bar T-shirt.

Caroline was arranging cereal packets in the middle of the kitchen table. She looked up at me and smiled.

'Morning, lovie. How'd you sleep?'

'Fine,' I answered quickly as I scanned the choices: Bran Flakes, Alpen, Shredded Wheat, Special K – ah yes, that'll do just fine. I shook a massive helping into a bowl, drenched it in milk and settled myself into a chair for a much-needed feed.

Caroline joined me, with her usual two slices of burnt toast smothered in raspberry jam.

'Did you find your room a bit chilly last night?' she asked.

'Not more than usual,' I said between spoonfuls of cereal.

'Well, my room was like an ice cube. Can you believe I ended up sleeping in my dressing gown? Think I'm gonna put on the heating early this year.'

For the first time in however long, things actually seemed normal. Caroline and I were alone, enjoying breakfast, no awkwardness, animosity or unwelcomed conversation. A decent selection of breakfast cereals accompanied by a milk carton that had been snipped open with care. Ah! The good life had returned!

'Morning!'

Ugh. Spoke too soon.

Jim was now hovering by the kitchen door, much to my overwhelming disappointment. He was already dressed (and dirtied, by the look of his grease-coated hands).

'Lovely weather out there,' he said, gazing out through the window above the sink. 'Gonna bring massive crowds to the Pleasure Beach today, I reckon. Good thing I'm starting my shift at four.'

'Aw. Lucky you!' said Caroline. 'I'm on just after 12.'

'Well, that still leaves a bit-a time to take a stroll round the town this morning. We could get a bite to eat, soak up a bit-a sun. Maybe Leon could come 'n' all. Watcha say, son?'

I stared down at my milky reflection in the bottom of my

bowl. 'No thanks, Jim.'

'Why not? Better than sittin' round 'ere on yer Tobler, now, isn't it?'

'Tobler?'

'Yeah, Tobler. As in Toblerone.'

'What?'

'You never heard the expression "Toblerone"? It's cockney slang for "on your own". Toblerone: on your own. Get it?'

What the hell was he on about?

I sighed. 'Jim, Toblerone isn't an expression. Toblerone is—'

'Yeah, yeah, yeah, I know all about Toblerones.'

The itching sensation around my elbows was intensifying. 'Trust me, Jim. You don't know the *first* thing about Toblerones.'

'Course I do! They're them posh chocolate bars that are always on special offer in duty frees. Stupid-looking things if you ask me. And a right nightmare to eat. You just try and break off one-a them spiky choccy pieces with your fingers, nearly snap 'em in two. Talk about shoddy manufacturing.'

Caroline could sense my tension levels rising faster than the Arctic sea levels and gave Jim a nudge. 'Eh, didn't you have something you wanted to show Leon? In the bunker?'

Show me something? In my bunker? Was this Caroline testing her skills as a comedian?

'Oh yeah, that's right!' Jim said enthusiastically. 'After you went to bed last night, I prepared a little surprise for ya down there. Wanna come see?'

'No, Jim. I don't. I want explanations. Starting with: how was someone given access to my bunker *without* my consent?!' I glared at Caroline like a bull seeing red.

'Leon, I *promise* Jim didn't touch any of your things, he just had a really great idea and, well, if say any more I'll ruin the surprise…'

Since when is having an idea a justifiable reason for breaking into someone's private space? Jim was well entitled to his ideas, so long as they were kept firmly shut away in his head and never let out.

'Don't be getting the lad too excited, love!' Jim laughed. 'All I did was fix the dodgy wiring.'

'*What?!*' I cried. 'You—'

'Hang on, son. Before you get your Twixes in a twist, just go down and have a look.'

'Go on, Leon,' said Caroline. 'I promise it's a good thing. You'll see.'

Then she winked at me. My own mother actually winked at me.

The two of them stayed at the top of the stairs while I walked cautiously down to the metal door.

I put the key in the lock, took a deep breath and turned it.

The bolt retracted, and the door opened.

A brisk chill raced past me as I stepped inside the bunker, pinching my skin all over.

No.

No.

No.

I looked over at the control panel on the wall.

4 degrees.

My priceless confectionery stash, which normally enjoyed a perfectly pleasant storing temperature of 18.3 degrees, was now in a state of hypothermic shock.

My legs started to buckle beneath me.

I fumbled around in the dark for a solid surface to lean up against, then suddenly the light came on. I looked over at the switch. Jim was standing beside it with a proud grin plastered all over his face.

'So watcha think, son?'

The cold was now catching in my throat. I couldn't speak, I couldn't move, I couldn't think. I was having brain freeze.

I'm a…

I'm a…

I'm a Twi—

Fudge it.

'Jim… *I* think… you're an imbecile! You are a hindrance to humanity! Not only have you obliterated my relationship with my mother and disrupted *every* aspect of my daily existence that I hold dear, you've also plunged my life's work into the equivalent of an ice bath!'

I raced back upstairs and pushed past Caroline, who chased

after me as I ran out the back door and down the garden.

In a frantic state, I tore through the passageways and tunnels of the funhouse until I reached my bedroom space, where I grabbed my sleeping bag and blankets, hurled them over the railings and watched them billow down onto the long grass.

By the time I'd rushed back down, Caroline was at the scene, trying to scoop up the covers.

'*Go away*, Caroline,' I warned.

'Leon, please just let me help.'

'I SAID GO AWAY!'

I pulled the covers off her, threw them over my shoulders and trudged aggressively through the grass.

The weight of the blankets bore down on my neck, forcing my head down, causing me to teeter from side to side as I tried to keep my balance.

Furious! Furious! Furious!! I was going to explode! Burst! Erupt! Denotate! This—

'Noel?'

I froze on the spot. Slowly, I tried to turn my head towards the voice, which made the covers slide off my shoulders to the ground, almost taking me with them.

Scribs was standing just a few metres from me. Beeboy was at her side. They both looked worried.

Scribs came a bit closer, gave me the once-over and tilted her head slightly to one side. 'All right, mate?'

My eyes narrowed. 'All right? Do I *seem* all right to you?' I said in an eerily calm voice.

'Well, not really,' she mumbled back. 'That's not exactly what I meant.'

The surging rage was just too powerful.

I took aim.

'Of *course* it wasn't. It's your badly wired brain, isn't it? *You* can't be blamed for not meaning what you say or jumbling words or saying complete and utter *Snickers* that you try to pass off as advice! I can only blame myself for *ever* having listened to your bogus wisdom, which has turned to be just as worthless as you!'

Silence.

Just the faint barking from a faraway dog and my heavy panting.

Scribs's eyes were welling up, but she kept it together.

'*Never* speak to me again,' she said. 'You got that? Never ring. Never text. Never call. Never knock. *Never* ever.'

Then she turned and ran away.

Beeboy hurried along behind her.

'Good riddance!' I shouted as they disappeared from sight. 'Good riddance, Tanya! Good riddance, Lawrence! Good riddance, Jim! Good riddance, Caroline! Good riddance, Glen! Good riddance, asparagus! Good riddance to the lot of you!'

33
Operation Wispa

(To be deployed in the event of a sudden decrease in temperature in the bunker)

1. Try to remain calm.

2. Tell Caroline to keep well away, unless it was her fault, in which case tell her to fudge off.

3. Stabilise own body temperature to avoid heat fluctuations when manipulating stash samples. Wear appropriate PPE-certified face masks and gloves; inhale and exhale from the nose only to reduce possible generation of condensation.

4. Remove stash from Pyrex drawer units and wrap each sample in thermal foil to ensure temperature stability. Place them on padded surface, preferably a duvet or other soft furnishing, in an isolated, unaffected space.

5. Increase thermostat by 0.5 degrees every 45 minutes to ensure gradual destabilisation of temperature until it reaches optimum temperature of 18.3 degrees.

6. Swab the exterior and interior of the drawer units frequently during temperature-raising process to remove any potential humidity molecules.

7. Try harder to remain calm.

The first twenty-four hours were touch and go, I'm not gonna lie.

I didn't think I'd manage to execute an operation of such scale and magnitude, especially one that I'd never trialled before (for obvious reasons).

It was crucial for me to keep my own body temperature regulated at all times, so if imagining the sight of me wrapped from head to toe in gold thermal foil like a mutant chocolate Lindt bunny amuses you, I couldn't care less. That's what it took.

Help is completely futile in moments like this. The best thing that anyone could do was to stay far, far away. Luckily, Caroline sensed this and sent Jim off back to whatever stupid bridge he presumably lived under. She then stuck a series of Post-its on the door of the bunker asking if I needed food, water, maybe an extra woolly hat? I ignored them all and just kept hiking up and down the stairs, ferrying almost three thousand vacuum-sealed packets from the bunker to my bedroom.

And don't think that it was simply a matter of just plonking the packets in any old space. First, each sample had to be individually wrapped in its own piece of gold thermal foil, then labelled using a white sticker and a black marker, so I could tell them apart. The samples then had to be arranged alphabetically in rows, to ensure that there were no sorting discrepancies. In the end my bedroom floor looked like an enormous tray of Ferrero Rocher.

Once the stash migration had been successfully taken care of, I got to work on slowly increasing the temperature on the thermostat. It was a painstaking job swabbing the inside of the Pyrex drawers after each temperature adjustment, and the tiny squeaking sound that the swabs made whenever they came into contact with a bit of condensation was criminal. *Criminal.*

That whole nightmarish part of the process took me a full two days, during which time I barely ate or slept. I even held off using the loo as much as possible. FYI, a fit-to-burst bladder is a great way of keeping yourself awake.

When Caroline caught sight of my heavy, bloodshot eyes at 11 p.m. on Sunday evening, she pinged off a message to Deluney saying that I wouldn't be in school for the coming days, due to feeling poorly.

Poorly?

As if!

I was in a semi-state of consciousness. I was barely existing. I felt like a hollow Kinder egg. An empty tin of Roses. I was a Freddo Frog bar with my caramel insides sucked out.

On Tuesday evening, at 9.36 p.m., the very last vacuum-sealed packet had been put back in the very last drawer.

I read the temperature on the wall for the billionth time and exhaled slowly: 18.3 degrees.

Order had been restored. Yes, the frosty enemy had finally been vanquished.

My body was in dire need of a proper night's sleep, but I

still felt the need to stay close to my stash. I must have had a touch of PTSD (that's post-traumatic stress disorder for those of you who've never experienced the Boxing Day crowds on the high street).

In the end, I decided to spend the night in the bunker, for peace of mind's sake. So, I brought down my sleeping bag, unrolled it on the cement floor and coiled myself up inside it. I found myself constantly staring up at the thermostat's small, lit-up control panel screen. 18.3 degrees. Still 18.3 degrees.

Just like the bunker, my emotions were now starting to thaw a bit. I was feeling a little less incensed. A tad less hostile. But don't carelessly read into that as if I'm saying that I was feeling remorseful for anything I might have said or done to anyone.

Why should *I* feel remorseful?

Exactly. I shouldn't.

Shouldn't I?

34
When Life Hands You M&Ms

'For the last time, Mr Crothers, you cannot demand a new set of questions on your specialist subject. Now please get out of the chair.'

'John, that last one was downright scandalous. It took you almost two minutes to read out the question! If you'd have just accepted my answer as soon as I'd said it—'

'Mr Crothers, this televised quiz show has been in existence since 1972 and I won't have a smart-arsed little brat like you dictating his own rules. All contestants must wait until I've finished reading the question aloud before answering. It's as simple as that. Now get out of the chair.'

'No, you get out of your chair.'

'Mr Crothers…'

'Swap it for a wheelchair.'

'Mr Crothers…'

'Or an electric chair – speed things along.'

'Mr Crothers!'

Ugh. That was an unpleasant wake-up call. Humphrys and

I have never argued like that before, even when I've accused him of mispronouncing words in German.

The clock face also made for unpleasant reading. 7.03 a.m. After just one night's sleep on a cement floor, my back had had enough. Also my legs were becoming twitchy and agitated. I was clearly suffering from some form of bunker fever.

A walk might do me good.

Yes. A walk.

And maybe an early morning bus ride?

That sounds like a plan.

I might just bring a snack with me, in case I get hungry.

M&Ms.

I'll take some M&Ms along.

A sharing bag of M&Ms, that'll do.

I don't need to waste time showering, do I? The clothes I slept in last night don't smell just yet. I'll just try and keep the sweating to a minimum.

Before you could say 'Galaxy Ripple', I was disembarking the 61 bus right beside a large orange brick complex which gave off a certain 'keep away if you know what's good for you' vibe.

The Harbour mental health hospital.

Yep. This was the place.

Luckily, the security guards out front were nearing the end of their shift and were in clocking-off mode. I just told them I that the devil was trying to take control of my body to orchestrate a world apocalypse and they waved me through. What a Pez take!

I didn't feel as confident when I reached reception, however: the lady sitting on the other side of the desk seemed very much awake.

'Good morning,' she said in a reassuring voice. 'Can I help you?'

Panic.

'Erm, Leon John Crothers, to see... Don.'

'I'm sorry?'

I leant in over the counter towards her. 'Look, here's the thing. I know that I'm not actually supposed to be in this place.'

'OK...' the lady said delicately.

' I just made up some mad story to get past your security guards out there. Seriously, how do you not feel a bit more paranoid with jokers like that on patrol? It's a good thing I'm not armed with a knife or have a bomb strapped around my waist. Anyway, I'm here because I need to speak with a lady who works here. Donna Asher. Do you know her? I know her because she's the mum of a friend of mine. Correction: mate. Correction: former mate – she recently cancelled our friendship. The truth is, I sometimes unknowingly say things that upset, anger or offend people. It tends to happen quite a bit actually. Do you know that some people get offended before I've even said anything? It's as if they're expecting to be offended. As if not being offended makes them feel like they're being short-changed or something.'

'Erm, have you come here by yourself?'

'So, it's kind of important that I speak with Donna. I would have called round to where she lives but I'm not allowed to call there. I've been told not to call there. Ever. But like I said, it's important that I speak with her. Now.'

'Has someone *brought* you here by any chance?'

'Like, I said, I need to speak with Donna as quickly as possible before I say something that's going to get me kicked out of here.'

The lady kept her eyes fixed on me as she slowly reached for her landline and punched in three numbers.

Uh-oh.

Please don't let them be 999. Please don't let them be 999.

'Hello, Donna, it's Carol here on reception. Erm, there's a young man at the desk who's just come in here by himself. He's saying his name's Leon.'

'Leon John Crothers.'

'Leon John Crothers. Eh, Leon would like to speak with you... are you able to come and... speak with him... now? Or... should I ask Declan and Raj... to escort him... to a waiting room... if you think you might be... a little while?'

Why is she speaking so slowly? That's just plain weird.

'*Really*? *Sure*? OK, I'll let him know. Thanks.' She put down the phone. 'Donna will be with you in a moment. Please feel free to take a seat.'

Oh, what a relief!

'Thank you. No *seriously*, thanks for helping me out. I *really* appreciate it. D'you know, I've met a fair few receptionists named Carol in my life, school and medical receptionists mainly, but I can tell you, hand on heart that you are definitely the most competent Carol I've come across. Kudos to you for actually doing your job.'

'Leon?'

I turned and saw Donna walking through a set of double doors beside the lift.

It was nice seeing her again.

She walked up to the desk, signed a few forms so that I could gain official entry and winked in what I can only assume to be feminine solidarity with the receptionist as she invited me into a nearby office.

We both sat down.

'Got to admit I'm a bit surprised to see you here, Leon,' she said. 'Is everything all right?'

'Oh yeah, fine,' I said. It was a half-truth but that wasn't for her to know.

I produced the bag of M&Ms from my rucksack. 'Thought you might find these useful, if you ever decide to dust off your old chopsticks.'

She took them from me and smiled. 'Thanks, Leon. That's kind of you.'

'They're about a decade or so old – that should give

you the edge you need. They're from my own personal stash, which I've just barely managed to bring back from the brink of destruction.'

'Tanya mentioned something to me about that,' she said. 'That must have been difficult.'

'Yeah, I'd rather not go into it. Mornings aren't the best time of the day for me to recall details. But I'm in the process of writing an in-depth report on the incident – I'd be happy to email you a copy once it's completed.'

She smiled again. 'Is there anything else I can help you with, Leon? It's just that I've got a meeting that's due to start in a few minutes.'

'Oh, well, there is just one other small thing: could you give these to Tanya when you next see her?' I pulled out another smaller packet of M&Ms from the front pouch of my hoodie.

'What are those?' she asked.

'They're a packet of limited-edition birthday-cake-flavoured M&Ms. Tanya once told me that she was quote unquote "proper mad keen" to try them ever since they came up in conversation when I was trying to educate her on the subject.'

'What subject?'

'M&Ms. Can you believe she actually thought that there were only *three* varieties? Original, peanut and crispy?'

'OK, well, I'll make sure to give them to her when I see her at home this evening. Do they come with a message?'

'What?'

'Well… is there any sort of message you'd like me to pass to Tanya with the M&Ms?'

Hmm.

I thought carefully for a moment.

'Don't eat them with popcorn.'

'Pardon?'

'Tell her not to eat them with popcorn. I caught her doing that once in school. She shook a bag of peanut M&Ms into a bag of popcorn. And then she ate them. Together. Can you believe that? It really irritated me.'

'OK… anything else?'

'Don't think so… unless you think it's worth telling her not to eat them with crisps? To be on the safe side?'

Donna nodded and mustered up another smile.

'Leave it with me,' she said.

35
The Trouble with M&Ms

A word of advice: M&Ms don't always make things better.

I know that now.

In hindsight I'm pretty sure that Donna knew that too when she was saying goodbye to me after our chat, but she was clearly keeping that secret to herself.

The next day, I went back to school.

Nothing had changed, really. The building was still ugly, the teachers were still incompetent, and Glen was still a psychopath.

There was one slight difference, though. Lawrence was keeping his distance. I might even go so far as to say he was avoiding me.

Well, *there*'s a role-reversal for you. Normally *I'm* the one trying to swat him away with my ruler or the back of my hand while he buzzes around me from the second I've set foot in the place.

I first saw Tanya as we were all piling into the classroom for our first lesson. She didn't acknowledge me when she walked in. She just kept a straight face and sat down in her usual spot, two desks from my right. During the lesson, I kept thinking that she was trying to get my attention, making a soft *pssst* sound, until I realised that it was just the geography teacher's lisp.

When the bell rang, she sped off back to her locker, without so much as an 'All right?'

Strange.

I was expecting her to be almost giddy to talk to me about the gift I'd sent her. Come on: limited edition *birthday-cake*-flavoured M&Ms – a flavour that has never been released outside the US, not even at the M&M World shop in London. What's keeping her?

Maybe she was just waiting until after the morning lessons, so we could speak together during the dinner break? That would make more sense.

Not quite, it turns out.

Despite me making the grand gesture of skipping my banana sandwich, banana and glass of milk to stay in Deluney and hang out with Tanya and Lawrence, among the noisy masses, they ignored me completely.

Seriously, what was going on?

Tanya couldn't still be in a mood about the other day, could she? If she is, then she's taking the Pez. *I'm* the one whose life has been torn apart, not her. And despite that, I still tried to be the nice guy and offer up an edible gift that she probably didn't even appreciate!

Maybe I should go and talk to her. Refresh her memory on

all things Mars and Murrie. That might help.

After the break, I loitered around Tanya's locker until she made an appearance to pick up her things for our next lesson.

'Hey,' I said.

No answer.

I think she pretended not to see me. On purpose.

I leant up beside the locker next to hers. 'Did you get the M&M's I gave to your mum yesterday?'

Still, no answer.

OK.

'Because Donna seems like a person that can be genuinely trusted, I'm going on the pretence here that you did in fact receive a gifted packet of limited-edition M&Ms yesterday evening. Did she pass on a message with them?'

'Don't eat 'em with popcorn,' Tanya said, scowling into her locker.

'Eh, right, except, now that I've had some time to think, I'm wondering if maybe that message wasn't the right message.'

She was angrily chewing on her bottom lip now.

'It would have been way better if I'd actually explained the significance that these particular M&Ms represent – you know, from a confectionery collector's perspective. That way—'

She slammed her locker shut.

I followed her along the corridor.

'Tanya, I'm sensing that you're not that keen to talk to me, which is a bit weird in all fairness, I mean, if we're both being honest about what happened on the weekend I was clearly the *real* loser in the situation.'

Tanya spun round. '*What did I tell you*?!'

'Uh, I dunno. Since we've known each other you've told me lots of things. When exactly along the timeline were you—'

'I said *never* speak to me again! You can't just show up when it suits you and blab on about whatever it is that you want to blab on about and expect me to just go along with it! You know the worst thing is, you don't even get it.'

'Get what?'

'How *bad* you hurt me! The way you can just carry on like that, without thinking for one second how what you said to me made me feel. D'you know, I never did feel all that good about myself, but thanks to you, I feel worthless. Proper worthless. So, job done. You can be proud of yourself. Now, leave me alone!'

The bell sounded for class and she disappeared off down the empty corridor.

My heart began squeezing itself tightly, the way Caroline squeezes a wet dishcloth over the sink.

'Goodbye, Tanya,' I said as soon as she'd turned the corner.

36
Acceptance

'Trish. *Trish*. Look who's walking in. I'm not dealing with him this time – you'd better take over.'

'Sorry, babes, I'm about to pop off for a bite to eat. Good luck!'

'Carol, I swear I'm not in the mood for it today. I'm already on edge, I'm telling ya! And of course, he won't have a flippin' appointment.'

'Leon Crothers to see Dr Snot. And no, I don't have an appointment, and no, I do not have an attitude problem and no, I will not call back another time when I've made an appointment and no, I don't care for the smell of your newly painted nails. Thanks to you, there's now enough formaldehyde in the air to embalm a corpse.'

'I'm outta here, Trish! I'm not having this! So, before you go stuffing your face, you'd better tell this one to get stuffed!'

The doc popped his head out of his office. 'Everything all right out here, ladies?'

'Nothing a petrol station tuna roll, a Diet Coke and a packet of salt and vinegar Quavers won't cure, Doc,' I answered as I invited myself into his office and sat down.

The doc stayed standing by the door. 'I'm sorry, Leon, but I don't have time to talk with you today.'

'Why?'

'Well, because *I* have an appointment with my optician to get new lenses put into my glasses. I'm due to leave shortly.'

'Shortly? Be more precise, Doc.'

'In precisely eight minutes.'

'Eight minutes! But that's... that's barely a quarter of a scheduled appointment!'

'And I take it you didn't schedule an appointment to come and see me, did you?'

'Only eight minutes! Are you serious?'

'Yes. Though I can't imagine that it would take a whole eight minutes to apologise for your outburst during your last unscheduled appointment.'

'Apologise? Who said anything about apologising, Doc? I meant every single word I said.'

The doc began putting on his coat. 'Would you mind closing the door when you leave, Leon? Thanks.'

Panic.

'OK, fine. In that case, here.'

I reached into the pouch of my hoodie and placed a handful of Jelly Babies onto the doc's paperwork.

The doc looked down at them suspiciously. 'More sweets, Leon?'

'Consider them a peace offering.'

'A peace offering? I don't follow.'

I huffed loudly and gestured to the doc's big leather chair. He took the hint and sat down.

'To mark the end of the First World War in 1918, Bassett's sweet-makers of Sheffield produced soft sugar baby-shaped jelly sweets in a variety of colours and called them Peace Babies. They are in fact what we now know today as Jelly Babies, though the official Jelly Babies branding only came into existence in 1953, when Bassett's relaunched the product after a temporary halt in production during the Second World War due to wartime shortages.'

'I see. And, erm, what am I supposed to—'

'Jelly Babies are often mentioned in the classic series of the television programme *Doctor Who* as a snack that the alien time traveller Doctor likes. They were first seen being eaten by the Second Doctor but they became most associated with Tom Baker's Fourth Doctor, who used to offer them to strangers to defuse tense situations (and, in one episode, bluffing an opponent into believing them to be a weapon). The Fifth, Sixth, Seventh, Eighth, Eleventh and Twelfth Doctors, as well—'

'OK, Leon, I get the idea.'

'But I'm not finished. And as a doctor, this should really interest you.'

'Oh, so I'm a doctor again, am I?' He held up one of the Jelly Babies, a green one, and stood it upright beside his stapler.

'I don't think you've grasped just how big a deal this is, Doc. I've been carrying those exact Jelly Babies around with me since I started nursery school! Not a word of a lie!'

The doc continued to stand the other Jelly Babies up alongside the green one in a crooked line. 'Is that so? And what's the reasoning behind that?'

'Oh, come off it, Doc, I'm hardly going to waste the remaining five minutes and fifty-one seconds probing that question.'

'Well, you'd surely agree that transporting decade-old Jelly Babies in your pocket in a ritualistic manner is not the kind of thing most people do, am I right?'

'Five minutes, thirty-eight seconds, Doc, thirty-seven, thirty-six... Let's get to the real point of my visit, Doc. I need you to sign me off school.'

The doc stopped what he was doing. 'Sign you off school?'

'Exactly.'

'Until when?'

'Indefinitely.'

'Why?'

'Why not?'

'Well, you know that signing a young person off school is very serious, Leon. I'd need to have a jolly good reason for doing so.'

'School's not my thing, Doc. I don't fit the mould. How is forcing my type into the system a benefit to anyone?'

'Leon, school attendance is compulsory in the United Kingdom for all children under the age of sixteen. Eighteen in most cases.'

'What about Charles Dickens, Doc? World-famous author – *Oliver Twist*, *A Christmas Carol*, etc. – left school aged twelve to work in a boot-blacking factory. Or Harry Houdini – dropped out of school aged twelve to work a variety of menial jobs including a locksmith's apprentice… that sure came in handy for his future escapist tricks that would make him the best magician of his era.'

'Leon—'

'Colonel Harland Sanders – didn't see through his primary school education because he had to stay home and cook for his family while his mum was out working after his father died. He later became the biggest drumstick of the fried chicken business.'

'Leon—'

'And speaking of drumsticks… The Beatles' Ringo Starr quit school at fifteen after finding out he was a dab hand at the drums during a prolonged stay in hospital—'

'*Leon*—'

'Walt Disney – quit school age sixteen. Former US President Benjamin Franklin – left school aged ten. Thomas Edison – only three months of formal education to his name, and he invented the lightbulb!'

'Leon, Thomas Edison's parents were both teachers. It's

true that he only attended a schooling establishment for a single semester, but he received a full education through home-schooling.'

'Oh, lay off the nit-picking, would you, Doc? Even Princess Diana didn't sit her A levels. Princess Diana. I think I'll turn out all right. And don't even think about saying something stupid like, "Ah, yes, but those were different times, Leon."'

'But they were.'

'Look, just do the honourable thing, would you, Doc? I promise if you sign me off school, I'll be on my way and never show up for an unscheduled appointment ever again.'

The doc looked down into his lap in silence for what seemed like forever.

Then, to my great relief, he began to nod his head.

'OK. As it is the honourable thing to do.' He extended his hand across his desk. 'Take care, Leon.'

'What are you doing?'

'The honourable thing. I'm refusing to sign you off school.'

'What?!'

'If I sign you off school, Leon, I'd be doing you a huge disservice in the long run.'

'And since when are *you* in a position to know what is best for me or not?'

The doc eyeballed me sternly. 'Leon, allow me to let you in on an important life secret: you don't control *anything*. None of us do. We might *think* we control most aspects of our lives, but sooner or later we are confronted with the unexpected. Sometimes the unexpected can be good, sometimes bad, often daunting, and yes, at times unfair. Very unfair, even. But there is one thing that we humans *do* have absolute control over. We control whether we accept this fact or not. Accepting that we cannot control everything, and that life is about making the most of what comes along, even the bad things, is what makes a crucial difference in how we spend our relatively short time on this planet.'

Wow.

I suddenly felt calm. Very calm. The crippling tension in my shoulders eased. It flowed right down my arms and off the tips of my fingers as I slowly reached out to shake the doc's hand.

I was still calm when I exited the building and stayed calm as I walked on the footpath alongside the after-school traffic that snaked right through the town. A light rain had started to fall, but I barely noticed it. The doc's words were still spinning in my head: *life is about making the most of what comes along… life is about making the most of what comes along.*

And would you believe that it was at this precise moment that someone unexpected *did* come along.

It was Lawrence. I spotted him out of the corner of my eye, hurrying down the footpath on the opposite side of the street where I was walking, trying to shield himself from the rain, which was now getting stronger.

I reacted fast and dashed out into the road.

'Lawrence!'

Cars started honking furiously all around me as I crossed three lanes of traffic. Lawrence glanced around and saw me but didn't stop.

I ran right up to him and blocked his path.

'Lawrence, good to run into you. Saves me the hassle of having to make an annoying detour.'

He made an attempt at a scowl.

'I… can't stop, Leon, it's raining and I not wearing my bee suit. I'm not protected. Also, I don't think I should be talking to you. You were really mean to Scribs the other day.'

To keep him from detouring around me, I quickly pulled off my hoodie and threw it over his head.

'Put this on. I'm due a shower soon anyway. Have you been speaking to Tanya? Has she been speaking with you?'

'Leon, I have to go. I'm on my way to a council assembly on local pesticide usage on communal green spaces. It's an urgent bee issue and I'm already late.'

'OK, in that case I'll be quick. Goodbye, Lawrence, it was nice knowing you.'

His face turned an even whiter shade of white. 'What? What do you mean? You're not moving away, are you, Leon?'

'I'm afraid so, Lawrence.'

'But why—'

'It's a very long story, Lawrence, but the condensed version is that we as humans have, contrary to popular belief, relatively little control over what happens in our lives. Did you know that? I couldn't control the fact that Caroline would take a fancy for that imbecile Jim, for example. But we can control how we deal with the unexpected. That's why I'm going to get my revenge on Glen tomorrow and get kicked out of school, thus steering my own destiny while I still can.'

'But… but why would you want to get kicked out of school?'

'So that Caroline and I can start a new life together. Far from here, far from Jim. Far away from Deluney. Far away from Tanya, who no longer wants to associate herself with me. I'm not sure where we'll end up exactly. Preferably somewhere with less seagulls. I really don't like those sinister-looking things.'

Lawrence began to hyperventilate. 'No. *No*, Leon. You can't. You… you just can't!'

'Yes, I can, Lawrence.'

'Stop calling me Lawrence! It's Beeboy. My club name is Beeboy!'

'Lawrence, there is no more club. There wasn't really ever a club, to be honest, I just was playing along.'

'You can't do this, Leon! You can't. You can't! Friends—'

In a move that was very out of character, I grabbed Lawrence's shoulders. 'Lawrence, listen to me. I know that having friends is really important to you, but having recently dabbled a bit in the concept, I've realised that friendships aren't my thing. I tend to function much better when I operate solo. Solo with Caroline, of course. But Tanya will still be your friend. That's something. Just don't act on anything she says, keep discussions light – the weather, etc. And if it makes you feel any better, I'm keeping the promise I made about taking care of Glen. After tomorrow, he won't be bothering you any more, and neither will I.'

My hands dropped down to their sides.

'Better let you get on with saving the bees. I promise I'll tell Caroline to plant some flowers at our new place. Not too many, though, and certainly none in hanging baskets. The last thing I want is to live in a house that looks like a country pub.'

Then I turned and stepped back out onto the busy road. The car horns helped to stifle Beeboy's calls.

'Leon! Leon!'

But I didn't stop. I just kept going.

37
The Fight (Prelude)

Green, yellow, red, orange, purple. Green, yellow, red, orange, purple. Green, yellow, red, orange, purple.

As I'd never actually started a fight before, I'd made a point of researching the subject online to see if there were any helpful tips floating about in cyberspace. Turns out there were loads. The big idea that kept popping up was the importance of mental preparation. To defeat the opponent, I needed to be mentally solid, focused, calm.

Many articles suggested listening to a song to get into the right headspace, but music really isn't my thing, as you know. Instead, I preferred to recite the different colours of classic Skittles in order of preference, keeping pace with my heartbeat as I headed to school on foot.

Green, yellow, red, orange, purple. Green, yellow, red, orange, purple. Green, yellow, red, orange, purple.

Another popular suggestion was the repetition of a motivational phrase to psych yourself up for battle. I found one of those too, courtesy of the prophet Noel (that's Noel Gallagher: Mancunian, dyslexic, holder of twelve UK number-one albums).

Green, yellow, red, orange, purple… I'm a man with a fork in a world of soup… Green, yellow, red, orange, purple… I'm a man with a fork in a world of soup…

I made my way through the school gates where grey polyester gangs were loitering around the yard. There was no sign of an Afro, but I did catch a glimpse of Lawrence, who gave me an unsure wave. He looked so stressed; the thought crossed my mind that he might spontaneously combust.

Green, yellow, red, orange, purple… I'm a man with a fork in a world of soup… Green, yellow, red, orange, purple… I'm a man with a fork in a world of soup…

Why isn't Tanya at school? She's *always* at school. Even though she isn't particularly brainy, she still seems prepared to get up every morning and give it a go. Maybe she's decided to cut her losses and eke out an existence in her room until she's old enough to fill out a job application for Starbucks. She'd be good at saying hello to people from behind a counter… maybe not so good at writing people's names on the take-away coffee cups.

Green, yellow, red, orange, purple… I'm a man with a fork in a world of soup… Green, yellow, red, orange, purple… I'm a man with a fork in a world of soup…

My eyes picked out Glen, skulking in a corner of the yard, by the bike racks. I steered myself in his direction.

Green, yellow, red, orange, purple… I'm a man with a fork in a world of soup… Green, yellow, red, orange, purple… I'm a man with a fork in a world of soup…

When I was just a couple of metres away, Glen caught sight of me.

Green, yellow, red, orange, purple… I'm a man with a fork in a world of soup… Green, yellow, red, orange, purple… I'm a man with a fork in a world of soup…

'All right, ass-burger?'

'Glen.'

'What you want?'

'I just wanted to tell you to your face, that while I'm flattered by the compliment, I'm not interested in seeking out a relationship with anyone right now.'

'You what?'

'Since I've started going here, you've been calling me ass burger… which I'm guessing is because you think that I've an ass… shaped like a… burger? Now while I personally don't have a problem with you spending most of your time in school leering at my buns, it does lead me to believe that you are trying to express some very strong romantic urges—'

Glen suddenly grabbed a fistful of my jacket, but I carried on unfazed.

'You'd better watch yourself, lad.'

'Sure thing, Glen. Gotta love that name: Glen. It really is the name of names. I guess you could say that it's the Big Mac of names.'

I was so focused on what I had to say that I was almost

oblivious to the fact that I was now completely encircled by goons.

'Fair dues to your folks for picking a name that reflects so many aspects to your character. GLEN: Ginger Lad with the Empty Noggin, Ginger Lad that's an Enormous Nutcase, then of course there's—'

In one swift move he hoisted me up off the ground and shoved me into the nearest wall.

My bladder briefly gave way. I was glad that I'd made the right decision of putting on three pairs of boxer shorts.

'Gonna break my nose without a camera crew present?' I choked as Glen's hand tightened around my Adam's apple. 'That's a wasted opportunity.'

'You're a cocky little creep,' he menaced. 'Do you have any idea what you've just walked into?'

'Do you have any idea how much you emotionally scarred my friend?'

He laughed. 'Ha! So, it's a revenge thing, is it?'

It was time to declare war.

'You. Me. After school. Round the back of Lakelands.'

His goons were now grunting with laughter.

'Fair enough.' Glen smiled. 'But lemme tell you somefing. If you don't show up, I'm not comin' for you. I'm comin' for 'im.'

He angled his head towards Lawrence. He was standing at the front of an impressive crowd of students who'd gathered a few metres from us. True to form, he had his hands over his ears and a distraught look on his face.

I was then released, but not before one of Glen's boys had rammed his knee between my legs. They left me writhing in a heap beside the bike racks.

The bell sounded and the crowd immediately dispersed.

Lawrence tried to help me up in a state of panic.

'Leon, Leon, are you OK?!'

'Nothing a triple change of boxers won't cure, Lawrence,' I assured him.

38
Defeat

3.57 p.m.

Three minutes to redemption.

Lawrence had been a nervous wreck all day, so much so that he was sent home an hour before the final bell, with crippling stomach pains.

3.58 p.m.

Two minutes and counting.

Lawrence was better off staying at home; at least that way he wouldn't be a distraction, or a liability.

3.59 p.m.

Strange how Caroline's been keeping her distance since Jim's cataclysmic air-con cock-up. I know that I told her in no uncertain terms to fudge off, but she usually makes an active effort to re-engage with me. No Post-its with my meals, no friendly wave through the kitchen window. Nada.

The bell sounded.

4 p.m.

It was time.

Leaving the gates of Deluney, knowing that I was never

to return, didn't have a massive effect on me. I was more concerned about how messed up my face was going to look in less than thirty minutes' time. That and anosmia. I have to say that while there are very few things that really petrify me in life, anosmia, losing your sense of smell and taste, is one of them. Apparently, trauma to the face or head is a primary cause of anosmia. The olfactory nerve brings the sensation of smell to the brain via the nose and is therefore at high risk of injury when there is trauma to the head.

That being said, there was no turning back now.

What was going to happen was going to happen. It needed to happen.

When I showed up at Lakelands a little after 4.15 p.m., the clouds overhead were filthy-looking. Great big snots of clouds. Glen was already there with his mates. There was also an intimidating crowd of students. When they'd copped that I was among them, they fanned out and formed a large circle around me and Glen.

It was all painfully clichéd.

I'd thought long and hard over the weekend about a strong, impactful one-liner to instigate the beginning of the fight, but Glen beat me to it. Literally. He simply stepped forward and landed a powerful right hook on my left jaw, sending me toppling into a load of spectators. Fresh blood warmed my mouth and I could hear blasts of noise from the crowd as my ears acclimatised to the blow.

'Up! Up! Up!' they were chanting. 'Up! Up! Up! Fight! Fight! Fight!'

Independent of my mind, my body obeyed, and I staggered back up to a standing position.

Glen was smirking at me with satisfaction. He probably saw himself as a cage fighter in a packed stadium in Vegas. What a donkey.

Still, I had to stick out this fiasco a bit longer to assure a legitimate school sanctioning, much to the disappointment of my ruptured lip.

I looked off into the distance as Glen stepped forward to take another potshot at my face.

Take it like a man, Crothers, I thought to myself. It'll all be over soon.

I was already beginning to see strange: a mirage-type scene was taking shape close by. It was as if I was staring at myself, dressed in my trademark yellow hoodie, walking across the green towards the crowd, head down with my hood up. It was shockingly realistic. Was I having an out of body experience? Had I in fact landed on my head when I fell?

Glen's knuckles suddenly blasted across my chin and I was once again catapulted backwards.

No sooner had I hit the ground than my doppelganger, who'd now reached the gathering, cried out in an all-too-familiar voice, 'Stop! Stop the fight!'

Lawrence?

What was he *doing*?

I somehow managed to get myself back to a standing position and tried to pick out Lawrence through the gaps in the crowd. Even from a distance I could see he was shaking like a leaf. His hands were practically vibrating in the pouch of my hoodie. He was also making some strange humming noise that got louder and louder as he pushed his way through the rows of interlocked shoulders towards the inner circle.

Glen burst out laughing the second he saw him.

Lawrence positioned himself between the two of us.

'Leon's not fighting you any more, Glen,' he growled. '*I* am.'

Now it was the crowd's turn to laugh.

Glen was loving it.

'What are you? His bodyguard?'

The bystanders whooped and applauded. Phones were held aloft to capture every cringeworthy second.

So, this was how it felt to be mortified *and* injured all at the same time.

'I'm *not* leaving here until one of us is on the ground, *Glen*,' Lawrence continued.

The crowd oohed loudly, just like in a shoddy pantomime.

Insane. Lawrence had gone completely insane. And now he was going to be beaten so badly that he might not ever recover. I had to do something.

I leant forward to pull Lawrence away from the danger zone, but I was manhandled by a couple of Glen's goons. They clearly didn't want to be deprived of a prime opportunity to witness bloodshed.

'Fists up!' Lawrence cried.

Glen had stopped smirking. He'd understood that he had an opportunity to seal his reputation in front of the entire school and he wasn't going to let it pass.

The crowd was now going crazy. 'Fight! Fight! Fight! Fight!'

The noise was excruciating. Worse than trolley wheels across a pot-holed car park, worse than wet leather shoes on creaky floorboards, even worse than the sound of someone speaking with a mouth full of baked beans.

Glen stepped forward with his fists gripped close to his jaw.

The crowd hushed as Lawrence moved a step closer and slowly removed his hands from the pouch.

Holy Snickers.

Bees.

His hands were covered with bees. *Hundreds* of live bees.

They hummed loudly in unison as they clung obediently to every square inch of skin from his fingertips to his wrists. It was the most terrifyingly spectacular thing I'd ever seen.

Lawrence raised his fists and lunged at Glen, who yelled some stuff that I can't repeat in case I set off the librarians, then he leapt out of the circle and scarpered from the scene.

The crowd went wild!

Cheering. Applause. Chanting. Selfies. Even more cheering.

I watched Lawrence take in the moment before shouting, 'Victory!' He punched the air with his fists, which sent a cloud of bees flying, and within seconds the entire crowd had frantically dispersed, leaving just the two of us.

My head was completely frazzled.

What had just happened? How could that have just happened? Did that really just happen??

I grabbed Lawrence and squeezed him like a tube of toothpaste.

'Lawrence, that was the most incredible thing I've ever seen! It was stellar! Sensational! Mind-blowing! I can't *believe* you managed to—'

Wait. Hang on.

The veins in my neck began to throb.

I stared into Lawrence's eyes, which were peeking out from under the rim of his hood. They were twinkling with happiness.

'Lawrence, *how* could you manage to do something so stupid?!'

His enormous smile deflated.

'Congratulations, Lawrence, you've saved the day. *Your* day perhaps but you've destroyed mine! And not *just* my day, but my entire life!'

'Leon, you're shouting,' he said, getting panicky. He started turning in circles and the bees on his hands increased their volume. 'Stop shouting. Stop shouting at me. I… I just wanted to help. I didn't want you to get in trouble and get hurt and get kicked out of school and, well, you're not a nice friend because all you do is complain that I don't do things right. I'm trying my best!'

'Trying your best? Thanks to you, Lawrence, I won't get expelled from Deluney, which means I won't be able to reorientate my destiny and will be condemned instead to this woeful existence until I waste away into adulthood and end up a deranged, homeless nutcase who talks to himself on park benches while he downs whisky and Maltesers – happy now?'

Fed up! I was fed up with all of this! I wanted out!

I stormed off across the green.

It felt as if everything was crashing down around me. I'd managed to find a way out but thanks to Lawrence's new-found courage and predictable stupidity, I had been denied access.

Now I was trapped. Forever.

There was nowhere to go, there was nobody to turn to... except... maybe I could swing by the doc's office? I was still on relative speaking terms with him.

I charged along on foot as the rain clouds menaced overhead, but by the time I'd walked the twenty minutes to the clinic, it had already closed for the day. There was nothing left to do but to keep walking pointlessly along the busy roads with no destination in mind whatsoever.

Right on cue, I felt the first drops of rain hit the back of my neck and within minutes I was drowned. I battled the deluge with hunched shoulders, avoiding the compassionate stares from onlookers who were warm and snug inside their cars as they passed me by.

Then a scruffy-looking blue Ford Mondeo pulled up alongside me and started honking ballistically. The driver's window rolled down and Jim's face stuck out from inside.

'All right, son? Hop in quick. I'll take you home.'

Unbelievable. Fudging unbelievable.

I ignored him and carried on walking, but he trailed beside me.

'Son! OI! Son! Do me a favour and get in the car!' he yelled through the passenger window. 'I ain't moving on till you get in!'

Cars were now beginning to form a noisy, impatient queue behind the Mondeo and some were joining in with Jim's beeping frenzy.

I eventually let out a howl of frustration, threw open the passenger door and dumped my sodden self into the front passenger seat.

'It's really coming down there, you're proper soaked, lad. Good thing I found ya.'

'*Found* me?'

'I spotted your little friend looking right sorry for himself when I was driving past Lakelands... what's his name again?'

'Lawrence?'

'Yeah, that's the one. Anyways, I pulled over to check on

him, and he filled me in on all that's being going on.'

'*Of course* he did,' I hissed.

'I wouldn't be too hard on the lad. He was just trying to—'

'Can you *stop* talking?' I snapped.

We drove on in silence along three kilometres of suburban roads until Jim pulled up outside my driveway.

'You back talking to your girlfriend, then?' he asked.

'She's *not* my girlfriend and that's none of your business,' I shot back as I reached for the car door handle.

'All right, just asking. She seems a nice girl, that's all. You really ought to sort things out with her.'

OK, that was the final straw.

'The fact that you now lay claim to Caroline does not mean you have the right to plod clumsily in and out of my life like some lost tourist!'

Infuriating, this was infuriating. My blood cells were now percolating furiously beneath my skin. I felt like a human jacuzzi.

'Listen, son, before you go, there's a couple-a things I wanna say.'

'No, you don't,' I said and pulled sharply on the car door handle, but his reflexes were quicker than mine and all the car doors locked in one click.

'As I was sayin', son, there's a couple things I wanna say.'

He manoeuvred himself around in his seat to face me, keeping a hand on the steering wheel.

'Look, first of all, I wanna say I'm sorry about the air con. Hand on heart, I didn't mean any harm, I just wanted to help and, well, we both know the rest of the story. I guess an apology isn't worth all that much to you now, but I still wanted to say I'm sorry.'

I rolled my eyes and huffed loudly.

'Second thing,' he went on, 'don't go off on the Lawrence kid for talking. He's just worried about you. So's your mum.'

'Oh, *please*,' I said, staring at the collection of air fresheners dangling from the rear-view mirror.

'Lemme tell you sommink, son: your mum's *whole life* is about you. You know the way she talks about you, it's like you're all she's got. I know that you getting kicked out of that school you're in would break your mum's heart, honest to God. Not because she'd have to move away to get you into another school, she'd do that for you in a heartbeat if she had to, but she'd be so upset with herself because she'd feel like it was all her fault. I'm no genius, but I'm thinking that you proper like this school you're in. You've got some mates, a nice girlfriend—'

'She's *not* my girlfriend,' I growled.

'All right, easy, tiger! Look, what I'm trying to say is that you getting kicked out of school and leaving your mates and putting your mum through all that because of *me*? I couldn't let a thing like that happen. I care too much for your mum. It ain't worth it for me.'

Is he? Is he saying he's going to leave Caroline? Is he

actually backing down?

'One word of advice before I go, son. Patch things up with your girl friend, yeah?'

'For the last time, she's *not* my girlfriend…'

'I never said she was! I said "girl friend", as in a friend who is a girl. I put a space between the words before I said 'em! Look, if you want my advice, and I'm sure you don't, I'd go patch things up with her. Friend, girlfriend, whatever, she seems like a keeper. There's my two and six worth, you can take it or leave it.'

'And just how am I going to do that when she said, and I quote, "*Never* speak to me again. Never ring. Never text. Never call. Never knock. *Never* ever."'

Jim let out a big 'HA!' and pounded the steering wheel with his hands like an excited gorilla.

'Is that all that's stoppin' ya? I swear you carry on like that, son, and you'll be right snookered when it comes to women, that's for sure!'

I honestly didn't have a clue what he meant. What does snooker have to do with anything?

'Look, son, saying sorry ain't easy, especially when it's a sorry with a capital S, but all I can say, having been there many a time meself, is speak from the heart and don't worry about her taking your apology. Just worry about what you're gonna say. If the words you say are the right words, then she'll hear them.'

With that, he unlocked the car door and I was finally able to flee round the back of the house, where I climbed up the funhouse's spiral slide and lay down on my sleeping bag.

Through the holes in the metalwork, I was able to make out a faint light shining out on the garden from the kitchen. I peeked through one of the holes and saw Caroline sitting at our kitchen table.

Was she waiting up for me? Had she seen me come in around the back? Did she even care?

She didn't look very happy.

Was she thinking about Jim? Was she thinking about me? About all the things I'd done and said?

In the end, I came to the conclusion that she was thinking about whether or not she could put a Fruit Pastille in her mouth without chewing it.

OK, so maybe it was a bit of a long shot, but at least it gave me peace of mind.

Seconds later, I was fast asleep.

39
In Noel We Trust

'Hello and welcome to a new series of Mastermind *with me, Clive Myrie. I am your new host and over the next thirty-one episodes, I'll have the privilege of joining ninety-six contestants as they—'*

'Hang on, hang on, what are you doing here? Where's Humphrys?'

'John Humphrys? Enjoying his well-earnt retirement, I imagine. Nice to meet you, Leon, I'm Clive Myrie, your new Mastermind *host. Shall we begin with your specialist subject?'*

'But Humphrys' final series hasn't even finished yet! We're only at the semi-finals! You can't just barge in here!'

'Well, it's your subconscious, Leon. I remind you that you have just two minutes to answer as many questions as you can on your specialist subject: The Unfriending of Leon John Crothers and Tanya Mackenzie Asher.'

'What? That's not my specialist subject!'

'Two minutes, starting now.'

'But—'

During their first altercation, in the halls of Deluney College, which stemmed from Tanya mistakenly telling a fellow classmate that Leon was an asparagus, what does Leon accuse Tanya of being?'

'This is a joke.'

'No, the correct answer is "stupid". How does Tanya initially respond to Leon during the same argument, when he lists off a number of examples that would lead him to believe that she is stupid, including no sense of orientation, slow to respond to questions and difficulty in grasping basic concepts such as his name?'

'You done?'

'Correct.'

'That was an actual question! I was asking you a question!'

'When Tanya tries to console Leon after the temperature in his bunker plummets to just 4 degrees after his mother's boyfriend Jim tries to mend a faulty lightbulb, she quickly flees when Leon shouts, "I can only blame myself for ever having listened to your bogus wisdom, which has turned to be just as worthless as..." what?'

'I'm not answering that.'

'No, the correct answer was "you" – "as worthless as you".'

'Oh, come on! I didn't say that! Did I? There's no way I'd say that to Tanya, Clive. You've taken that statement way out of context. Humphrys would never do a thing like that! Never!'

My eyes sprang open.

I checked the time. 1.58 a.m.

It was hard to work out if the luminous grinning clowns staring down from the ceiling were mocking me or trying to cheer me up. It didn't really matter anyway, it wasn't going to change the fact that I was wide awake at two in the morning, or that my urge to sleep wasn't coming back any time soon.

Only four hours to put in until daylight. That shouldn't be too hard.

I started off by ranking present-day popping candy brands by order of excellence in my head. The result was as follows.

Popping candy brands by order of greatness:

1. Aftershocks
2. Pop Rocks
3. Fizz Whizz
4. Brain Lickerz
5. Tango
6. Sparx

Then I considered an answer to the following question: if one chocolate bar had to disappear off the face of the earth for being completely pointless, which one would it be? Of course, the answer had to be Drifter bars – what an absolute waste of cocoa solids they are. If only Nestlé would read one of the sixteen letters I've previously sent them on the subject and take the hint.

That packed in about twenty minutes. Then I decided to

roll over onto my stomach, so that I was lying face down on the floor with my eyes closed, and imagined that I was dead, and that the flat surface touching my nose was in fact the lid of my coffin. I do this quite a bit when I'm awake in bed at night. Sometimes I like to lie in that position with my eyes open and pretend that I've been mistakenly buried alive.

As the minutes crept up towards 3 a.m., more serious questions were starting to make their way to the surface:

1. Why does eating asparagus make your wee smell funny?
2. Will I ever manage to fit an entire Terry's Chocolate Orange in my mouth?
3. What could I say to Tanya to have her be my friend again?

I spent a good while thinking about these questions but didn't manage to come up with anything.

Then a thought came to me.

What about Noel?

What would Noel Gallagher answer to those questions?

The asparagus one's easy. He'd just say, 'Why isn't it compulsory for headlining acts at Glastonbury to actually know how to hold a guitar? Why would anyone say that they support Man U? Why anything?'

Noel probably could stick a whole Terry's Chocolate

Orange in his mouth, if he wanted to. He's got that invincible nature about him. But he'd more than likely say, 'How much of a plonker would someone have to be to do a thing like that? Do I look like my brother Liam?'

And question three? Just what would Noel have to say about question three?

I wonder.

Then suddenly, the answer came.

Within minutes I was up, dressed and straddling the saddle of Caroline's bike, which, through a stroke of pure luck, she'd left propped up against the shed.

The cycle to Tanya's took a few minutes longer than usual and a bit more leg effort because the front basket of the bike was loaded up with my portable stereo.

When I reached Bethany Crescent, still in the pitch black of night, I set myself up under a lamp post on the side of the building that Tanya's bedroom window looked out onto. I cranked up the volume, inserted her Oasis *Morning Glory* CD and fast-forwarded to track three.

The song's first chords had only just been strummed when windows up and down the complex began to light up.

As the dense echoes of accompanying cello joined in, curtains parted and heads stuck out from windows.

'What the hell are you playing at?!'

'Shut that crap off!'

I was too nervous to look up at Tanya's window. It'll be

just my luck that she's off staying at her nan's or joined a missionary and buggered off overseas.

Then suddenly…

'Oh, my gawd! Tans! Look! It's that racist little mate of yours!'

My heart jumped.

I looked up. There was Tanya, her mum and sister and a tall, broad man that I guessed was Dev.

Tanya didn't show any emotion on her face – she just stared back at me as the song cried out about winding roads and blinding lights and things that were impossible to say.

'Tans! Tans! Is this kid in love with you or what?' her sister yelled.

That was my cue.

I dashed across the crescent and tore up the open-air concrete staircase, slab by slab, while Noel's lyrics spurred me on, reminding me that Tanya was the one.

She was always going to be the one.

I reached her flat and banged on the front door. It swung open wide to reveal four stunned faces.

'What are *you* after?' said Dev.

The problem was, I was completely out of breath.

'I… eh… I wanna… phew…'

I threw my head between my knees and searched desperately for oxygen.

'I've come to… I want to… say…'

'What?' cried Denise. 'That you're in love with our Tans?!'

'God, no!' I blurted out. 'Ugh! You've got it spectacularly wrong! There's a surprise! Almost the entire English-speaking population has misinterpreted the lyrics to "Wonderwall". *That's* why I've come up here. Everyone, and I mean *everyone* thinks that "Wonderwall" is a song about a person declaring their love for someone, when in fact it's *nothing* to do with that *at all*. Poor Noel is sick to death of explaining that in media interviews.'

'Ya what?' said Denise.

'"Wonderwall" is a song about an imaginary friend who saves a person from themselves. That was the message. That's what Noel Gallagher wanted to say when he wrote those lyrics!'

'So?' said Dev.

'So what?'

'So, what do *you* wanna say, then?'

Panic. Stress. Panic.

'Eh… well… what Noel said. Yes. Ditto to that.'

The four of them scrunched up their faces.

'Ditto to that?' Denise tsked. 'You serious?'

I looked at Tanya.

Come on, brain, get it together.

Say the right words. Say the right words and she'll hear them.

'Tanya, I'm sorry. I'm really, really sorry. I know that me saying sorry isn't going to change how you feel about me and what I said, but I want you to know that, as far as friends go, you deserve better. Way better. You probably know that already, you're clever like that, but I just wanted you to hear that from me. You deserve a friend who's as great a person as you are, someone who makes you feel as good about yourself as you make them feel. You deserve a friend who isn't self-centred or obnoxious or rude… although just to clarify, I'm not racist. Really, I'm not. Well, not on purpose anyway. You deserve a friend who accepts you for who you are, who always has your back. Someone who makes you feel like, despite your faults, you are a person of value. That you are worth something, even if most of the time you don't feel like that at all. I know that I don't deserve any more chances, but if someday you ever were stupid enough… actually, forget the word "stupid"… erm… willing to let me try and be the friend that you truly deserve, I'll try my hardest. Promise. Though I should probably be honest and say that even if I do try my hardest, it's highly unlikely that I'll ever be as good at being someone's friend as you, because… you… you… uh, I bet this is why Noel kept things a bit vague in the pre-chorus. How *do* you explain to someone that they've saved you as a person? It's impossible!'

I stopped rambling and looked into Tanya's eyes.

She looked straight back at me.

A tear rolled off her cheek and dropped onto the floor.

Oh fudge.

This wasn't supposed to happen.

What the hell do I do now?

Run, Crothers. The answer is run.

So that's just what I did. Downstairs, someone had already shut off the music. I slung the stereo into the bike basket and pedalled away.

Cycling home was like an out of body experience. All my senses were numbed. My eyes didn't register the marbled orange and pink hues of the early rising sun, like a bowl full of Fruit Salad Chews; I couldn't hear the clicking of the bike chain as I changed gears, or the first chirps of early rising birds. I couldn't smell the dew from the grass or the spearmint flavour from my gum.

I had shut down. The fire in my heart was well and truly out.

'Serves you right, ya little idiot,' I'm sure Noel would've said.

40
Conversations With Mum

I was woken up late the following morning by what sounded like giant talons shredding metal off the roof of the funhouse. I poked my head out between the railings on the second floor, expecting to see a pack of ravenous vultures impatiently waiting to tear scraps of meat from my chest. Turns out it was just a flock of pigeons, which was fairly disappointing. It would have been so convenient to have it all end quickly like that. Painfully, sure, but at least it would have been impressive.

Maybe I could trap one of the pigeons on the roof, kill it and eat it raw? That would finish me off. Pigeons are riddled with bacteria, especially round these parts. On second thoughts, maybe not. The news headlines wouldn't be very flattering: *Local boy dies from eating pigeon*… people would probably think that I'd eaten a pigeon because I just wanted to eat a pigeon and therefore assume that I'm as thick as a plank.

Maybe rats were the answer? I could just drop down into the sewers underneath the Blackpool Tower and wade through the pipes until they stumble upon me. Northern rats have a reputation; some say they even outrank London rats in size and stealth. A Blackpudlian rat isn't afraid to leap onto your face and wriggle its flabby, furry body into your mouth to try and gnaw off your tonsils. If I managed to locate a nest in the sewers, then the whole thing would be over in a jiffy. And the headlines would be brilliant: *Boy dies after being consumed by swarm of killer rats*. I'd just have to find a clothes peg to shield myself from the pungent smells of the sewers and a Post-it to inform Caroline of my plan so that the emergency services would have a point of departure when the time came to locating my corpse.

I went back into my makeshift bedsit, threw on my hoodie, jeans and trainers before chucking myself down the spiral slide. As I reached the bottom, I realised that something was blocking the exit. I dug my trainers into the plastic to slow myself down; the squeaking sound was unbearable. I came to a halt just centimetres from a multi-coloured mound of wool.

Caroline?

What was she doing here? And why wasn't she moving?

'Eh, you're blocking the exit,' I said awkwardly.

She turned around very slowly and looked me. My arms and legs were stretched out in all directions in the sloping tunnel like a spider ready to pounce.

Without saying a word, she got up to let me pass and then sat back down again. Her rings clinked delicately off her ceramic *Keep Calm and Carry On Knitting* mug.

This really wasn't ideal. If Caroline had decided to plonk

herself on my turf, then it meant that she was angling towards a chat. And I really didn't want to waste my time pretending to seem concerned with whatever it was she wanted to say. I had an obituary to draft.

'Jim told me what happened yesterday,' she said as I went to step off the metal stairs.

'Well, there's a surprise: Jim sticks his big beak into everything… all the time…'

'It's a good thing he did; I got a call first thing this morning from the school. Apparently, you'd picked a fight with a boy in your class after school and another boy got involved with handfuls of bees, or something like that? The headmaster's been taking calls from irate parents all morning.'

'For the record, Caroline, there's a lot of important details you've skimmed over in that summary—'

Caroline gripped her mug tightly. 'So, Jim is *that* bad a person that you wanted to get yourself expelled so that you and I could get as far away from him as possible?'

'Your words, not mine.'

'I'm not saying that any of this has been easy for you, Leon, but the truth is that Jim means well. He tries to do the right thing.'

'If you say so, Caroline,' I said. 'I'm going up to the house to grab a Post-it and a clothes peg. Then I'm heading out.'

'Are you going to do the right thing?' she asked.

'What do you mean?'

'Are you going to apologise to Tanya?'

My heart spasmed.

'We're not friends any more, Caroline.'

She looked up at me, shielding her eyes against the morning sun. 'Well, that doesn't surprise me.'

'Since when are *you* well-placed to take sides on a situation for which you don't even have the full context?'

'You called her worthless, Leon. Whatever she did that upset you, I'm sure she didn't deserve to be called worthless.'

'For your information, I *did* try and apologise, not that it should concern you in the slightest.'

'You apologised, Leon? *You?* Well, what happened?'

'Were you listening, Caroline? I said we weren't friends any more.'

'Are you sure you apologised, Leon? Because you can sometimes—'

'Yes, I did! I apologised and she wasn't having it. So that's the status quo. We are no longer friends and I'm much better off as a result.'

'And why's that?' Caroline asked as she finished off her tea.

'Tanya doesn't see things the way I do. She's the complete opposite to everything I am.'

'That's not always a bad thing, Leon. D'you know there's that famous saying: opposites attract.'

'What a load of Snickers. Opposites don't attract, Caroline, they repel. They clash. And that's exactly what happened

271

between myself and Tanya. She was encouraging me to be just like her, which I'm not. I was expected to be a Twizzler, when I'm in fact a Toblerone. It's no wonder catastrophe ensued.'

'What was that, Leon?'

Uh-oh. How did I manage to let *that* slip out?

'Nothing, Caroline. I'm off.'

I went to leave, but Caroline grabbed the back of my hoodie and gently pulled me down to the step she was sitting on.

'Explain please, Leon,' she said.

'Explain what, Caroline?'

'Eh, that you're a *Toblerone*?'

'There's nothing to explain. Forget it.' I tried to stand up, but she held on tightly to my sleeve.

'Toblerones have little sticky chewy white bits mixed into the chocolate, don't they? Is it something to do with that?'

'Nougat, Caroline, those sticky chewy white bits are nougat. The Toblerone bar was invented in the late 1800s by Swiss confectioner Theodor Tobler. Toblerone comes from his surname, plus "torrone" – an Italian word for a type of nougat.'

She thought for a moment. 'Is it that the triangle chocolate pieces are shaped to look like mountains? Do you have a thing for mountains?'

Oh, good grief.

'The shape of a Toblerone *does not* represent mountains! Why does everyone think that? The shape is meant to represent dancers from the Folies Bergère — a cabaret music hall in Paris.

The dancers would form a pyramid at the end of the show, hence the triangular shape of the chocolate.'

'You can't have a go at me for thinking that, in all fairness, Leon. There's a huge mountain on the wrapper.'

'Well, in that case, I'm sure you'll be surprised to learn that there's also an outline of a bear on said mountain, which FYI is actually a depiction of the Matterhorn, the twelfth highest peak in Europe.'

'A bear? No there isn't.'

I sped back up through the funhouse labyrinth, grabbed my 'in case of emergency' Toblerone from inside my sleeping bag and brought it down to show Caroline. She stared closely at the packaging.

'Gosh! I never even noticed that! Why a bear?'

'A bear features on the Bern coat of arms. Bern is the town in Switzerland where Theodor Tobler was originally from. The historic Toblerone factory is based there and was also the location where the title sequence of the original *Willy Wonka & the Chocolate Factory* was filmed in 1970, but the less said about that the better.'

'So, is that it, then? You're like a bear?'

'No, Caroline. I'm as much a bear as you are a pelican.'

She thought for a second, then snapped her fingers. '*I've* got it. It's that you're complicated.'

'What?'

'Remember what Jim said about Toblerones being

complicated to eat? He's right, you know, it can be a right hassle trying to break off a piece of Toblerone without your wrist aching or chipping a tooth. May I?'

She opened up one end of the cardboard packaging, tipped out the spiky chocolate bar and tried her best to break off a chocolate triangle peak.

I watched her struggle for a little bit in amusement before I moved her hand to one side and, using my finger, pushed the chocolate triangle gently in the opposite direction. It snapped off with ease.

Caroline's eyes widened in amazement. 'Oh my God. How incredible is that? You made that look so easy!'

'Very misunderstood things, Toblerones,' I said, looking across at her.

She turned and faced me. There was a sappy look in her eyes, which was fairly offputting, but for the purposes of 'plot closure' I'm supposed to dress it up as being a tear-jerking, meaningful moment where a mother and son come to a sort of unspoken reconciliation.

Let's just say it was awkward as hell, but it did the job.

'We'll work it out, Leon, OK?' She sniffled through her smile.

'Whatever, Caroline. Are you going to eat that Toblerone now?'

'No. Why d'you ask?'

'You've opened up the packaging, so you're going to have

to eat it now.'

'Well, no rush on that, is there, really? I can always pop it in the fridge.'

'Don't even think about it, Caroline. My life's already messed up enough as it is; a Toblerone in the fridge is likely to push me over the edge.'

Up nearer the house, the long grass rustled.

Caroline stood up from the steps. 'Looks like you have a visitor.'

What?

Who?

I stood up and squinted down the garden.

Tanya was standing right there in the middle of the grass.

Caroline waved to Tanya to come over, then whispered to me, 'I'm going to make myself scarce.' She tucked the Toblerone under her arm.

'Where are you taking that Toblerone?' I asked.

'Not to the fridge, Leon, message clearly received.'

'No, best leave it here with me.'

'Leon, I just said that—'

'I heard what you said, Caroline – I'm not deaf. I'd just rather keep the Toblerone with me.'

'Why?'

'To show Jim. Will he be around today?'

'Maybe. Would you like me to call and ask him?'

'Whatever, Caroline.'

She smiled and nodded as she headed back up to the house, saying a quick hello to Tanya as they passed by each other.

My intestines were tied up like a sailor's knot.

'All right?' she asked.

I shrugged my shoulders.

'Same here,' she said.

Then she reached into her coat pocket and pulled out the packet of M&Ms I'd given her.

I shook my head. 'No, it's OK, you can keep those.'

'I wasn't planning on keeping them.'

'Oh, right,' I said, extending out my arm.

She reached out and took hold of my hand.

Wow.

It was the craziest feeling: like an electric current had just passed between the two of us.

'Why don't we share 'em?' she asked as she sat us both down on the steps.

My head was all over the place, I was completely lost for words.

Tanya sensed that I was struggling. 'D'you know what? I've got a better idea: I'll eat these, and you can tell me all about them.'

'*Really*?'

'Yeah. But you've only got a few minutes till Beeboy shows up. I told him to be here for eleven. Think you'll manage?'

I looked over at her and smiled.

'I'll try,' I said.

Conclusion

You'd think that by now, after forty chapters, I'd have managed to escape the wrath of the editor's wagging finger.

No. In the poncy world of publishing, that's not how things go.

Apparently, you need to bring the story to some sort of 'definitive conclusion' to 'mentally and emotionally satisfy the reader'.

After hearing that, my own personal conclusion was: what a load of Snickers.

So, here's my conclusion:

Hello again,
My name is Leon.
I'm in the Asparagus Bunch.

Goodbye.

A note about the autism and dyslexia representation in this book

While this book is based on my own lived experiences with autism, I did draw on important support from the UK's National Autistic Society when addressing autism in this story. Though there are common challenges that autistic people share, autism is a spectrum condition and affects people in different ways.

The advances that have been made these past decades in understanding autism have been substantial, during which time, different diagnostic labels have been used, such as: autism, Autism Spectrum Disorder (ASD), Autism Spectrum Condition (ASC), classic autism, Kanner autism, pervasive developmental disorder (PDD), high-functioning autism (HFA), Asperger syndrome and Pathological Demand Avoidance (PDA). Based on recent changes however to the main diagnostic manuals, Autism Spectrum Disorder is likely to be the most commonly given diagnostic term, according to the UK's National Autistic Society.

The problematic history surrounding Hans Asperger has provoked widespread debate within the autistic community. Indeed, today, many people whose profile fits that of

Asperger syndrome are being diagnosed with Autism Spectrum Disorder instead.

That being said, every person is different and should feel comfortable in choosing how they wish to identify themselves. Those people who have an Asperger syndrome diagnosis may well choose to keep using the term, whereas others may prefer to refer to themselves as autistic or having an Autism Spectrum Disorder.

Dyslexia is a learning difference that also occurs on a spectrum; some people are mildly affected and others more severely. Everyone with dyslexia is different but there are commonly shared difficulties with reading, spelling and writing and related cognitive/processing difficulties.

Jessica Scott-Whyte,
Paris, May 2022